ADAM TS CONLON

# Young Tiger, Mad King

*A Wolves of War Story*

**PRIVATE DRAGON**
Publishing

*Dedicated and Special Thanks to Ron Fair,*
*Who helped build Fangaard, the Holy Lands, and Kendala*

# Contents

# 1: Three Kings

In a hall of stone and wood, King Archibald Hŭdáshī, second of his name, sat upon a high-backed chair within Kendala's Gate, flanked by a steward and his personal guardian, Tedge da'Żern.

His hands held the heavy, bald head of Alej ha'Qíj. His wide eyes stared into the equally unblinking, glassy orbs of his former commander. The mouth hung open with a horrified look.

Three nights since Tourm retook Southport.

Three nights since the Tourm-men screamed, "*Unbreakable.*"

Three nights since that dishonorable cur—the one for whom the people cheer—threw ha'Qíj's head at his feet from high atop his night-black warhorse.

They did what they could against the Unbreakable, but it was no use. They had come after him with spears, but his warhorse was too fast. He easily battled fire and water dancers with ungodly ease.

And why not?

He *did* kill ha'Qíj, great useless oaf that he was.

*But vengeance shall yet mine be.*

He would indeed make the Tourm-men pay for their insolence. He would make them scream blood and spit their own shite from their mouths.

"Of all the Kendalans we had to leave behind, at least the Unbreakable was kind enough to give me your head. I shall make certain your family adds something of you to their shrine. And then, I shall have my vengeance against Tourm."

*How?* asked the head.

"Oh, I have ideas." He hoped to still hold Southport before putting them into effect.

"I know the horse and rider, ha'Qíj. They fought at Zachwalaç when Tourm first came to Kendala. The Unbreakable had been a soldier in that small sortie. That giant was there as well, a human siege engine, tossing Kendalans about like ragdolls."

*It was a bad day for Kendala*, said the head.

"Our ancestors wept with us."

Archibald stared deep into the decaying head. "Our defeat matters not, ha'Qíj. 'Tis the Unbreakable. 'Unbreakable!' The Tourm-men roared it rhythmically, as if a song, over and over as da'Żern and I fled."

2

*Can't you see why?* asked the head.

"Oh yes, it is quite clear why this insect of a Tourm-man was called the Unbreakable. He had survived the skirmish outside my gates. He survived the sortie when the Tourm-men's camp was discovered, survived the ambush awaiting them at Seagate. He destroyed their camp, retook Statek, and reunited so very many Kendalans with their ancestors.

"But ha'Qíj, he was not without his scars." Archibald sneered. Cuts slathered with ointment, misshapen nose freshly broken, moving as though fire pained his body. "You *broke* the Unbreakable, didn't you?"

*The Tourm-men do not call him 'Unbreakable' because he is invincible.*

"No. He is Unbreakable because no matter what you—or anyone else—did to his body, they could not destroy his spirit."

Archibald closed his eyes and pressed ha'Qíj's graying forehead to his.

"When I was a boy of four or five, Grandfather told me something I'll never forget. 'You cannot crush fire.' On the night of his funeral, I found a candelabrum. I wetted my fingers with my tongue. I remember how the flames tickled as I pressed my thumb and forefinger together, releasing from the wick a thin trail of blue smoke.

"'You lied to me, Grandfather,' I thought. But when I was ten, I

3

saw lightning strike a tree. Fire grew. Flames ate the crackling bark, burning it, blistering it.

"That is what he meant. The Unbreakable is no mere candle's flame. He would consume all. He is a wildfire that, if left to burn, could ignite others of Tourm, perhaps even Kendala. Orrick the Unbreakable *is* a fire that cannot be crushed.

"But his survival means one thing, ha'Qíj. Crossing the Sea of Trees is manageable. By the looks of that foolish sortie, they had not many supplies. They survived by their wits and cunning.

"Thus, shall I send *my* army through the Sea of Trees. And Tourm, with their vehement dishonor, king grown fat through indolence, shall never see us coming! After all these years, ha'Qíj, mine ancestors will be appeased, and vengeance shall be mine!"

He gripped ha'Qíj's head, body reeling with pleasure. He imagined Orrick the Unbreakable, broken; face smashed, arms and legs disjointed, body riddled with cuts and arrows.

The thought excited him to no end. His eyes popped open, aware of the painful hardness in his trousers. After placing ha'Qíj's head on the floor, he commanded da'Żern, "Fetch me that Ninnish slut."

Expressionless, da'Żern raised his hand and the steward dashed from the hall, returning moments later with the girl in tow. Face plump and riddled with pockmarks and acne, hair brown sticky with sweat. His men sought her for pleasure whilst in Southport, and he must have interrupted their activities, for she came to him with skirts disheveled and breasts bare.

Cautiously, she approached him. "I'm grateful ye summoned me." Her eyes immediately sought his tight trousers. "An' I can see why! Lemme take care o' y'."

"Silence," said Archibald. "You are but a bestial rag."

"Oh, I can be quiet," she replied. "Some o' the men taught me t' use my mouth."

Without even awaiting his response, she dropped to her knees and went to work undoing the lacing of his britches.

"Kill her."

The slut's eyes went wide. She found his unblinking eyes and saw her mortality within. Then da'Żern's cicada wing ripped through her flesh, exiting her sternum betwixt her breasts.

Da'Żern withdrew his weapon and her body collapsed, blood pooling on the cold stone floor.

Archibald stood and redid his laces. He contemptuously eyed the slain slut. "Do not presume to speak to a king, even if you are satiating his mortal desires."

His frown deepened when the corpse did not answer.

"Da'Żern!"

The Grand Forest Dancer who impaled her—with red skin and fine black hair—stepped forward. The armor he wore was of bronze. A cape of virescent silk flowed down his back. He held his double-bladed weapon, the cicada wing, at his side.

"Your Eminence?"

Archibald cast his gaze over the slut once more. "Remove her from my sight. Give her back to the men. Tell them they can use all her holes—including those freshly made. When they are finished, put the body on the wall of Kendala's Gate."

"Yes, Eminence."

Da'Żern bowed and called forward two guards. They gripped each of her lifeless arms and dragged her from the room. Blood trailed in their wakes.

"Thank you, da'Żern."

"It is my pleasure to serve His Eminence."

There was a moment of silence that Archibald could not abide. "Da'Żern?"

"Yes, Eminence?"

"Do you know why they call Orrick *the Unbreakable*?"

The Forest Dancer bowed his head. "He's strong and willing to sacrifice himself to attain his goals."

"But I've a name too, have I not? I was called something when I took Southport unawares, when the people of Statek ushered into their homes like frightened cattle, their women and children given to appease the voracious appetites of my soldiers?"

"The young tiger."

"The young tiger," he repeated.

The words tasted good in his mouth. He was the young tiger, the scimitiger of House Hŭdáshĭ of Kendala. The prowler in the forests and fields, the devourer of beasts and children and strong men. But was he *Unbreakable*?

Archibald sunk back into the hardwood chair and sighed. "Orrick might be unbreakable, but Tourm is not."

"Do you have a plan?"

"I do. I shall see my men through the Sea of Trees and into Tourm once more. But this time we shan't start with the southern portion. This time we march into the very heart of Tourm, to the Great White Fortress!"

"How? Forgive me for saying so, but the city is walled high with white marble and limestone twelve inches thick. 'Twas designed to be impregnable. Can we truly make for it?"

Archibald looked to his steward. "Wine." The steward bowed and went to the cellars. "All cities fall, da'Żern. Just as every

7

mail has a gap, so does every wall. I'll send mine army through the Sea of Trees, siege engines through Durwyn's Pass."

"Forgive my insolence, but will that be enough?"

"It *must*, but I've another—"

"Your Eminence!"

Archibald stood from the abruption. The steward ran toward the throne. In his hands, he grasped no wineskin or chalice, but behind him was a falconer. Seated upon her heavy glove was a raptor with beautiful plumage blue and green. A crest of silver feathers, like springtime flowers, sprouted from her head.

"A seahawk," Archibald marveled. "This is joyous indeed! Just as I was about to mention it to you, a seahawk is come from the Stonehill Empire! 'Tis as though 'twas sent by mine ancestors!"

The steward and falconer bowed to him. Then the steward ran back toward the cellars to complete his original task.

Archibald greeted the falconer, giddy as he examined the creature sitting upon her arm. He did not care that this was not the passenger pigeon he had initially sent.

"Read the letter," he commanded. "What is Bosker's response?"

The falconer undid the string to which a tube of parchment was tied. Upon it was indeed the seal of House Reign: a noble, albeit wingless, dragon that stood on four legs was stamped upon the

8

break in teal wax.

Da'Żern received the tube, broke the seal, unrolled the parchment, and read:

"*My good King Archibald,*

"*How good it is to hear from you. Your struggles are not in vain, I hope. When we heard of your attempts to reclaim what your neighboring nation had taken from yo—how they slighted your good and ancient name, how they balked and sent men to attack you without warning—our hearts could not help but stir.*

"*I and my council should like to hear more from you, about your kingdom and the struggles you face before we make our decision to aid you with our naval fleets. Please, come when you can. Allow Keeper to remain in your custody. When your departure nears, send her back and we shall know when you expect you.*

"*Respectfully,*

"*Bosker of House Reign, the Seventh of His Name, Sovereign of Stonehill, Emperor of the Holy Lands.*"

"He answered!" Archibald cried. "This is a joyous occasion!"

"No doubt Stonehill will host you gladly."

"Thank you, da'Żern. Your words are kind." He looked past the falconer and the Forest Dancer to see the steward coming with a pewter chalice. He sunk to one knee as he handed it to him.

Archibald took the cup and raised it to his lips—but he stayed from drinking. His mouth twisted into a frown. With a swift motion, he kicked the steward under the jaw. The wretched boy flew backward, landed on his back. His eyes were bewildered as he searched for answers.

"Did you not *see* how happy I was? Did you not *know* what good news we received? We've a seahawk from Stonehill, you impudent chattel! They wish to discuss the use of their naval forces!"

"I only—"

"How dare you only bring wine for me, and none for da'Żern or the falconer? You foolish insect, how did I ever conclude that you were worth any more to me than a corpse?"

Bewilderment turned to fear. "Your Eminence?!"

He looked at the steward sourly. Then his eyes met da'Żern's. There was no need for words, no nod given. The Forest Dancer thrust his weapon's long, thin blade into the steward's throat. He rasped and gagged, choking on the blood pouring out of him.

Da'Żern pulled the blade free from the steward. His head hit the ground, wound pumping blood in slow, small spurts.

"We've had a bloody morning," said Archibald. "Let the soldiers have the steward as they have their Ninnish slut, then put his body on the gates with hers."

He returned to the hardwood chair and said, "Falconer, no doubt this bird is Keeper. Find a haven for it in the aviary. We make for home at dawn tomorrow."

"Yes, Eminence," the falconer said with a bow.

As she left, Archibald sipped from the chalice. He recoiled, and his mouth tightened from the bitterness. "What *swill* fills my cup and stains my tongue?"

Da'Żern looked to his sides. "May I?"

Archibald stared into the dark red liquid, viscous and disgusting. He nodded. Da'Żern took the cup and sipped from it. His mouth tightened.

"And it is—?"

"An Ianth red."

"Ianth?" he asked, indignant. "Did this come from one of the barrels we took from Tourm's Gate?"

"It did."

Archibald threw the chalice. Metal clanged on the stone floor. Wine splashed into blood.

"If that fool steward wasn't dead already, you'd kill him again! Idiot!" He spat at the pool of blood and wine, the two now indiscernible. However, the body was already out the door, dragged by the same two guardsmen that took the slut.

The King leaned back, swallowed hard. Not even gracing these dusty stone floors with his saliva rectified the bile building in his throat. "Run, da'Żern, and pour me another cup. Bring one for yourself as well. We shall toast to our eventual victory."

Da'Żern bowed and left the hall. Both blades of his sword pattered red droplets onto the gray floor.

Archibald frowned as he watched him go.

*The men are disheartened, fatigued from running, and saddened by defeat. The Tourm-men struck a critical blow, but all is not lost.*

The knights guarding the doorway had returned, but it mattered not. "Are you proud, Grandfather?" he prayed. "I cannot crush fire. But I *can* crush stone, bones as well. Does that not please you, Grandfather?"

*It does, my boy.*

"Oh." He slipped into the hardwood chair, reclining into its uncomfortable, splintery arms. But he did not care. "Good. And you aren't angry with me, Grandfather?"

*Angry at what?*

His voice dropped to a whisper. "I killed your son, *my* father. I'm a kinslayer."

*He was weak,* Grandfather answered. *He was naught but a contemptuous old man content to let his kingdom—his soil—be held by those ungodly savages, the Tourm-men. I've told you this time and again.*

Archibald's eyes shut tight. He put his hands over his face and bowed his head. It was better this way, better to see the ghosts that spoke to him. And what a surprise, for his grandfather's wrinkled face, indeed appeared in the darkness. He wore robes as white as the heavens, smiling kindly behind his white, wispy beard. Gone were the puffy, flaccid scars left behind by blood pox. Eyes twinkled sincerely, without malice.

"And the others?"

*The others are proud as well.* His voice was as crinkled as autumn leaves. His hand extended, and Archibald felt his grandfather's warmth upon his shoulder. *They are happy to know that you are finally righting the wrongs done by Tourm. Worry not, for we shall help you. We shall be ever at your side. We shall walk ahead of you, protecting you. We shall flank you should you need carrying. We shall even walk at your back to alert you to your traitors.*

*And remember,* said Grandfather, his smile now gone, *all men are traitors. But they needn't be judged so swiftly. Even traitors are useful. 'Tis when they outlive their usefulness, they must be slaughtered for the swine they are.*

"Like the slut and the steward?"

*She was too comfortable. He, too stupid. If your servants cannot*

13

*know your thoughts and whims, they are unfit to serve you. Is that not true?*

"You told me that when I was a boy."

*I did no such thing. But I tell you it now. You'll be wise to remember it to the end of your days. If they cannot know your thoughts and whims, they are unfit to serve you. This is not true of only your servants but of all people: lords, whores, knights, peasants, servants, and even your own wife and children when you come into them.*

"And what of my—" He choked on his words, suddenly worried. "What of my ancestors?"

A second face appeared in the darkness, with graying hair and a long, jowly face that still smiled with kind eyes. He too wore a white robe.

"Father," Archibald gasped, awed.

*Are you worried still about killing me?*

"I am, Father."

*Be not. I am* glad, *for you will bring peace to our realm, honor to your family. And when you join us, your name will be sung in heaven as though you were a god yourself!*

Archibald's tears leaked through his tightly shut eyes. "Thank you, Father!"

*Thank me not yet. It is how the world works. We are your ancestors, those that came before you. Yes, you slew me, but what does it matter anymore? Kendala now belongs to you.*

Archibald smiled. He was about to say something more, but his Grandfather intervened. *Our time grows nigh. When we return, we know we shall be even happier with you as King of Kendala.*

The ghosts of his father and grandfather faded from the blackness. He looked up toward the sunlight, which spilled in through the high windows. Tears dripped down his cheeks, wet and happy.

He would kill his enemies, and all the traitors—even those in his own service. And he would make his ancestors so very proud.

# 2: The Crypts Of Spire Black

As the procession rode into Zachwalaç City, Archibald opened the curtains of his litter and saw the dusky, rosy sky dusted with stars. His eyes lazily passed the legion of guards protecting him and he looked to his magnificent city, where the high walls and two-pronged tower, both built of black stone, loomed in the distance. Their path took them over hills where rice paddies stretched for miles. Men and women, young and old, with sun-browned skin had only just finished their mundane chores and prepared to journey back to whatever sinkholes they came.

Once inside Zachwalaç's gate, peasants and beggars shuffled to the side as their horses ambled down the streets. The slums were filthy, the streets ran wet with urine, and the inhabitants stank of offal. The people, thin and misshapen as branches, looked at him with hungry eyes and dirty mouths. They dare not approach him with so many soldiers amassed.

*Would that I could kill them all, burn the slums down*, he thought. *But you cannot crush fire.*

The slums' dirt roads soon became cobbled paths. The buildings stood prouder here, less decrepit, and contained far fewer rats.

Spire Black—named Czarny Wideleç in the Holy Tongue—stood in the center of Zachwalaç, rising from the loam like a devil's sword. The outside of the castle was as shiny and black as obsidian, but inside the stones were hard red and marbled white.

The cavalcade stopped at the moat surrounding the tower. Now dried, it contained pits with broken shafts and iron spikes upraised like the quills of a skinmiller bear.

A bugler's trumpet bade the drawbridge descend. In the gate-house, his litter-bearers lowered him. Da'Żern appeared from behind the thick curtains and offered a hand.

Archibald stood and looked around, happy to be back in his homeland. Surrounded by soldiers and stewards, he entered past the black vestibule and into the enclosed bailey.

Hanging on the walls around him were portraits of kings long dead. They appeared dignified and stern. Many lived to see their hair gray, some even white.

Archibald had spoken with each one of them—and some nights with more than one. They whispered traitor's names into his ears, told him to conquer for Kendala. When he awoke the next morning, drenched in a fevered sweat, he called for his guards to uproot those named traitors. He had them killed publicly, in the city square.

*They should know not to cross me*, he thought. *But no matter how many are killed, they never learn—*

"Welcome back, Your Eminence."

Archibald turned to find his castellan, ka'Vín, a portly man with strong arms and a squashed nose to match his short neck. His head was bald, but a wispy white side-beard traveled down past his jowls to his shoulders. He wore the same barrel-shaped spear-mail as his other soldiers, but his was coated with silver, shrouded with a cape of violet silk.

"Ka'Vín, how good of you to greet me. I trust you know of our failure."

The castellan already had a wide mouth, and it seemed he could stretch it more when he frowned. His eyes, though steely, were walled. *It makes him look like a toad in regalia.*

"We were glad to learn of your victories and most upset when learning of your defeat. But you yet live and I understand we still hold Tourm's Gate. Are we giving up?"

Archibald eyed him, curious. *I've had no dreams about him. None of mine ancestors have spoken to me about treasons of late, especially not of him.* "We quit not Tourm, but indeed were driven back. Our aim is restoring honor, and honor has not been restored."

"Do you have a plan?"

"A seahawk is come from Stonehill. They would meet with me in person. Should this go well—as I know it is destined—we nigh shall see the end of our conflict against Tourm."

"Stonehill," grumped ka'Vín. "And what piece of us would they have in return for their generosity? Their ships and soldiers shan't be free."

"*I know that, you mailed toad!*"

Soldiers and stewards stopped their unpacking to look at them. Archibald fumed, his fists shook against his legs. "I should not have shouted. The troops shall amass and head through the Sea of Trees. We shall send siege engines through Tourm's Gate, ignoring Nin."

"Then—"

"Our objective is Albion." Archibald cracked a smile. "It shall be a surprise attack."

The frown deepened on the castellan's face. "Do you believe our men can survive the Sea of Trees?"

"That *Unbreakable* Tourm-man did. Are we not better than him?"

The little toady looked around nervously, which made Archibald frown.

*Clearly, he has no answer.*

"You *fool*! We are better than Tourm-men. If they can, so too can we. And they'll not expect it, either."

"As you say."

That blithering fool bowed, and Archibald smiled.

*The time of your end is at hand, castellan.* "You've displeased me. Da'Żern!"

The red-skinned Forest Dancer, cicada wing in hand, stepped forward and bowed. "Eminence?"

"Kill the castellan."

Da'Żern hesitated if only for a second. *He might not think I saw, but I did.*

He raised his dual-bladed weapon and struck out, but the castellan slapped the blade away. Then he drew his own ornate, tasseled sword.

Da'Żern stretched his left leg out, bent on his right, and with both arms held the cicada wing in front of him, vertically. "Remain still, ka'Vín. 'Tis naught for you if you continue resisting."

"Da'Żern, why do you listen to him?" the castellan pleaded.

"Our king has commanded your death. I need not like it, but I must comply. So must you, ka'Vín."

The castellan spat. "You've your weapon raised against me, but it should be against *him*! He commands these daily executions!

He commands us war with Tourm! This is madness—even you must see it!"

"You *are* a traitor," said Archibald, eyes gleaming. *All men are traitors*, Grandfather had said. "Da'Żern, kill him for treason! I command it!"

"Do not listen to him, da'Żern!" ka'Vin groveled. "Let me pass!" While he crept backward, da'Żern edged forward.

"Why?" asked da'Żern. "If you escape, you might run to Tourm. We cannot have that. Your only way to freedom is through me."

"You're *right!*"

Ka'Vin lunged, sword outstretched, not at da'Żern but Archibald, himself.

Da'Żern, however, was quick as a mantis. With a stroke and clashing steel, the castellan's sword went spinning away. Da'Żern twirled and struck six times with both straight blades—*or was it ten or twelve, or more?*

The number was inconsequential. Now ka'Vín wore a face full of cuts, bleeding red. His skin peeled to reveal the rubicund meat underneath. With a final strike, straight and true, da'Żern sent one of the crescent-shaped blades on the shaft through the castellan's throat.

The fat old toad dropped dead, bleeding out onto the red-and-white stones.

21

Archibald smiled all the wider. "Excellent, da'Żern. You are a Grand Knight indeed."

"Your praise honors me," da'Żern said, dropping to a knee. "But Castellan ka'Vín was a fat old man, not fit to govern your castle in such trying times. The victory truly is yours."

"*Mine?*"

Da'Żern remained kneeling, eyes averted. "With your heavenly judgment, you saw it was time for a new castellan, one smarter and stronger to protect your stronghold during these most trying times. Nigh at hand is your journey to Stonehill. Soon too shall many soldiers wander the Sea of Trees. Our castle needs protection now more than ever. A new castellan was imminent."

Archibald chuckled, pleased. "Your words are a kindness, da'Żern. But ka'Vín's disturb me. Do you think me *mad?*"

"Most men could only dream of the honor of House Hŭdáshī, Your Eminence. Is it madness to wish to restore honor? Instead, I say glorious. Your wishes, your commands, your mission: glorious one and all."

"Rise, da'Żern. Send word to Duke Wobbegong to prepare a ship. *King's Glory* shall do. We have a long journey ahead of us. But first—"

Da'Żern turned to two soldiers and shouted, "Put ka'Vín's body parts on the walls!" Then he beckoned a steward. "Mop clean this blood!" Lastly, he turned to Archibald and bowed. "I make my leave now, Eminence."

With a swish of virescent silk, the Forest Dancer made for the rookery.

Next, Archibald sought his enchantress general. She often liked to reflect and meditate in the quartz garden. Many did, but Archibald preferred the crypts beneath Spire Black. Still, he must meet with her. So, he walked through the courtyard, down a small alleyway, to where huge quartz boulders jutted from the ground, shining in waning sunlight. Waterfalls sprang from sluices over formations crafted by the finest masters. Hanging ivy climbed the walls and bamboo pierced the ground. Flowers of all shades bloomed around the stone path.

There, an old woman stood, looking into the ruddy sky. Elbow-high, her body the color of burnished gold. Her head was rid of all hair, her bald pate wrinkled and laden with brown spots. Veins seemed prominent on every visible part of her, as if they yearned for their escape from her withering body.

"Yü'Róna." His enchantress general.

Using a cane, the wizened woman hobbled forward. Her mouth broke into a smile, revealing only three brown teeth. Her voice creaked like loose stones. She had her quirks, and indeed was the oldest thing in Zachwalaç, but she was astute. Archibald counted on her counsel as much as Father and Grandfather had.

"Happy to have you back," she wheezed.

"I shan't stay long. Stonehill calls me away. Da'Żern prepares a passenger pigeon now, telling—"

"Forgive me, but I heard. Castellan ka'Vín is dead and you soon make for Bugross Bay."

"*How?*" asked Archibald.

"I have made it my duty to know Spire Black's workings since I was a young maid."

*She frightens me, but she is no traitor.* He recalled his grandfather's words. *Well, at least she is good about not revealing it, unlike the others.*

"Thank you, yü'Róna."

She eyed him. "You could use some peace after your journey. Remain here. Reflect. Meditate. Besieging Southport ended unwell."

"I know what I must do."

"I promise, what you *must* do doesn't include rushing into another fray so soon."

Archibald narrowed his eyes. *Damnable, useless woman.*

"You remembered to bring the dead back with you?"

"We did what we could," said Archibald. "And ha'Qíj's head."

"My herbalists shall prepare them for their families. Such a pity. Those who can receive parts for their shrines, shall. Those who cannot—well, I'm more than happy to bless their figurines."

"You do them a kindness, yü'Róna. And I believe I will meditate."

She smiled toothlessly and hobbled away.

*Da'Żern spoke true. Ka'Vín was getting too old for his position, and he was my father's man besides. The selfsame can be said for yü'Róna.*

Archibald would meditate, but not here. He made for the crypts, deep below Spire Black.

Taking a torch from a sconce, he descended the narrow passage-way, which continued down for a quarter-mile.

Down at the bottom was the undercroft of Spire Black. Cobwebs and heavy dust made gray the once red walls. Stone pathways were built over the underwater lake. Stagnated water rankled the air and wrinkled his nose. *But it is not far now.*

At the end of the passageway was another hall, more cavernous than the keep, tombs all in rows. How blessed was he that all his family was intact?

Smaller houses and families' shrines contained their deads' teeth or mummified fingertips, distributed through children, siblings, and sometimes parents.

25

Commoners may receive ashes, the lowest and most impure idol. Those with no family were most dishonorable and tossed into pits, unnamed and forgotten.

But, if a soldier died in a foreign land, or a sailor at sea, and the body could not be returned, an enchanter would bless a figurine. It was between pits and the fragment. At least the family had a symbol of their ancestor to pray to.

*How many Kendalan families would receive these figurines?* He frowned. *Too many.*

Archibald felt fortunate, though, for the wealthiest families had crypts or mausoleums, where the remains were kept completely intact. Spire Black's crypts displayed his ancestors' remains in their entirety, up to the very first king.

He strolled amongst the tombs, eying their names. He placed the torch in a sconce near the entranceway, took a seat amidst the ruins of stone, crossed his legs, and closed his eyes tight.

"I am returned to Spire Black. I ask you now, mine ancestors. Speak true and impart your guidance on your faithful son."

In the darkness, he could hear the faint sounds of water, rats scurrying across the stone floor. His eyelids tightened. "Speak to me, Grandfather. I need your aid!"

He did not know how long he remained inside the walls scratched by ghosts. The ground was wet and cold beneath him, and the night airs sent drafts even this far below the castle. Did minutes pass, or hours, or even days? He remained undisturbed and would do so until he had his answers.

"Grandfather, please!" he begged, eyes still tight. "Kings Qelín, Aún, Tą́ś, answer me! I beseech you, souls of my soul! I entreat with the Stonehill Emperor soon and need your guidance. Please! Where are you when your humble son needs you most?"

*Not everyone wishes you well*, a voice said. It crept into his mind, born on tendrils of darkness—darkness darker than even his shut eyes could offer. "Rą́d?"

The voice oozed contempt. *Who else would it be? Were it not for your underhandedness in the paddy pools that night, I'd yet live. The throne would be mine, and Father would still be king!*"

"Father *wanted* to die, Rą́d! You saw not his face, heard not his nightly whimpers!"

*How could I when I was dead by your hand*?!

Archibald's eyes snapped open. In the darkness, he stood, a boy of nine dressed in a robe of black. His face was bloated and purple, his features distorted as if underwater. His limp, wet hair stuck against his face. His eyes were black emptiness, staring. His puckered mouth sucked air like a fish.

"No!" Archibald attempted to crawl away, but his legs could find no strength to stand.

*Yes*. The mouth puckered still. Somehow this long-dead child

27

could project himself into his mind. *I am returned. I have not forgotten. You wanted me to show you the rainbow fighters. Why you chose the middle of the night, you thought I'd never know. But I did know as soon you plunged my head under the shallow water. I knew when you held me there until I stopped kicking. Alas, I knew too late.*

"What do you want of me?"

*Revenge. I want you to know, we are not all of us happy or proud. Father is blinded. He knows better than to speak against the King. But do you believe he wanted to die? Is that what he told you? Were those moans in the night truly him?*

"Yes! He has told me himself! He said that death has brought surcease from his suffering! He *promised me*, Rąd!"

*He promised you after he was dead*, said Rąd. *But I know you're a murderer. More than that, I know you have not what it takes to claim Tourm. Your siege against Albion will fail. You will be captured, tortured; your death will be slow. And when you die, finally, you'll meet me in the Under Realms.*

"*NO!*" Archibald shrieked. He turned around, bare hands gripping the stone floor as he struggled for escape. But the boy's sickly voice was all around him.

*Yes*, sneered the boy. *I will be waiting for you. Father and Grandfather will be with you when you sail on* King's Glory—

Archibald was already in the next room. He shrieked again

when Rąd appeared before him, blocking his exit. He stepped backward, looked to the stagnated water.

"Bring them back!" he cried. "You're the reason none show this night! What have you done with them?"

—*I shall sail with you, too.*

His laughter was deep and booming. Father's laughter. It bounced off the walls to reach his ears. Archibald shrieked and screamed as Father's laughter became higher, like the laughter of some unholy child.

Archibald's face pressed against the damp stone walkway. Tears spilled from his eyes. Long after Rąd was gone, he remained. Awake—*ever and always shall I be awake*—to the sound of water, and the echoes of the unknown.

# 3: Commons The Urchin

The litter waited within the gatehouse, ornate with gold etchings and curtains of scarlet silk. Four long yokes extended outward, two in the back and two in the front, and one solder for each. Backs straight in their barrel-shaped spear-mail, weapons by their sides. Da'Żern was among them. So too was al'Foyl, a Grand Water Dancer. These two were Grand Knights, the highest office of knighthood in Kendala. The other soldiers meant to accompany them were merely peons, not worthy to be addressed by him and certainly not worthy for him to remember their names.

Archibald climbed into the litter, relaxing amongst the plush pillows of jade green, ruby red, and royal purple. He left without a word to yü'Róna, did not mention that his elder brother, Rąd, long since dead, appeared to him, had not seen his grandfather since his vision in Kendala's Gate.

Somehow Rąd kept the other kings from him. He relied on their judgment to rout out traitors. It had not happened in a sennight, and soon the people would think him soft.

He tried not to think of it, but Stonehill, instead. With their navy,

Tourm would be naught to him but grist in the wind. Then Rąd would be silenced for good—no! *Then shall he admit I am the true king—the king our ancestors wanted, that our dynasty deserves!*

Smiling, Archibald looked at the spear-bearing soldiers, and then to the baggage and supply trains that would see the journey to Bugross Bay.

Archibald sat in the direction of travel. The curtains swayed as the litter rose from the strength of the four porters that surrounded it. With uncomfortable unevenness, he bobbed side to side. He frowned at the motion and hoped his men would steady themselves in time.

They did not. Instead, after a good amount of time, the rocking intensified. Yelling sounded outside the silken curtains. One of the porters shouted back.

Before Archibald could ascertain the commotion, there was a grunt. The front right side of the litter collided with the ground, snapping Archibald from his position. A fight ensued. Spears plunging wetly. Men groaning. Archibald adjusted his cloak and peered from the litter.

Da'Żern and al'Foyl had their weapons in hand. One of the porters was face down, arms and legs limp. Blood pooled near his head, as well as near the heavy stone that suffered the man his fate. Archibald licked his lips and saw the soldiers facing a small rabble of young men.

He saw the muddy streets, smelled the acrid air. *The slums.*

Whilst the other soldiers battled with the dozen or so peasants, da'Żern stepped forward and threw one of them to the ground. He was filthy, his skin dark, his arms thin, his eyes wide and uneven in direction. His black hair was matted to his head and upon his lip were the makings of a mustache. The lad was younger than Archibald, which came as a surprise. But the King feigned calmness and looked to da'Żern.

The Forest Dancer spat. "This boy assailed Your Eminence's litter. He threw a rock at Gord's head. I know not his state." Da'Żern put his foot onto the back of the boy's head, no doubt filling his mouth and eyes with piss and mud. Then he poised his cicada wing high.

The dozen young men ceased their attack if only momentarily. When they saw their friend was in danger, however, they no longer wished to fight with the guards. Instead, they wished to save their friend from his certain punishment. They shouted and scrambled but were only met with a human wall.

Da'Żern smirked, his teeth painfully white within his sun-red face. "Grant me his death. We are pressed for time, but I will make it as bloody as possible."

Archibald raised his hand. "Stay, da'Żern. Lift him up that I might face him."

*Again, he hesitates.* But da'Żern did it.

The lad's face was coated in mud, making him smell as offal. Blood trickled from his nose and above his left eye. Curious, the dozen others ceased their clamoring.

Archibald scrutinized the urchin. "Why assail my litter?"

Silence.

"*Boy*! Why did you assail your king's litter?"

Silence still, and Archibald frowned. "Da'Żern, from him do pluck an eye—"

"Because you're a bad man," the boy mumbled. "We saw your litter return. We knew you'd leave again."

"You attacked me because I rode through your slums?" Archibald smiled. "That seems hardly justified."

The boy grimaced. "You don't want to help us. We watch as you take the farmers' foods, as those others worry for money or food. We are cold in the wintertime, eating bog-rats from the rice paddies—"

Archibald raised his hand limply. Surprisingly obedient, the boy quieted. "You are in want of food. I am in want of something else. You attacked my litter, damaged my soldier and *I* stand accused of injustice?" His eyes narrowed. "What is your name?"

"Markí."

"Markí," Archibald repeated, tasting it. "It sounds to me as though you want justice. However, *you* stand guilty, witnessed

33

by mine own eyes!"

The urchin winced. That made Archibald smile. "Your last name, Markí?"

"I am an orphan. Most of us are. We cannot find work. You—"

Again, he was silenced by a flaccid wave of his hand. "Become a knight for me, Markí."

Da'Żern's mouth fell agape. "Your Eminence?"

"Don't play games!" the orphan shouted. His eyes welled, his voice broke.

"I play no games. You want for warmth, shelter, food. More than that, you want for purpose in this life. Very well, so shall you have it—and so shall your friends. Spire Black has a mess hall for soldiers, who are well-fed."

The orphan looked around, confused. "You want me—us—to become soldiers?"

"Is there any reason why not?" Archibald looked to the fallen porter. "You've impressed me with your stone-throwing." Mud slipped from Markí's face in clumps. "Hark well on my words, lad. I'm certain Da'Żern wouldn't mind the other—"

"I will," said the orphan.

Archibald grinned. "Wonderful! A warrior you shall indeed be."

He looked to the crowd of boys, still beaming. "And you! Will you not join your brother?"

"Is this *wise*?" asked da'Żern.

"They need food and shelter. I need soldiers. Or did you so soon forget how *the unbreakable* oppressed us?"

Da'Żern's lips puckered. "I did not forget."

"I did not expect you had." He looked back to the lads behind the soldiers. "Your friend has made an honorable soldier of himself. Will you not do the same?"

The lads hesitated. *How I hate servants that hesitate*!

But finally, one boy said, "I will." And then the others followed his lead.

Archibald smiled wider. "Do you now see, da'Żern? They only want to be treated as human beings and I have given them that."

"Yes, Eminence."

"Good. Escort the children to the castle. Let Castellan ha'Ÿun find them beds in the barracks and food in the mess hall. All, that is, but Markí." The King turned a knowing eye to the boy, and he withdrew. "He shall accompany us. And do hurry, da'Żern. The longer you take, the later we grow."

Castellan ha'Ÿun was everything that da'Żern had suggested

in a castellan: young, robust, faithful, and competent. The young Fire Dancer had proven himself, indeed, and truthfully, Archibald only cared about the last: competency. If the castellan could punish whomever the King wanted punished, whenever the King wanted them punished—*without hesitation*—then he was good enough for his title.

*Ka'Vín had failed in that. So too had that steward in Kendala's Gate. I fear da'Żern treads the path as well. I count twice that he has hesitated to kill when I commanded it. Once more and he shan't be able to hesitate again.*

Archibald waited within his litter while da'Żern returned to the castle with the rest of the filthy flock. He demanded a skin of tiger bone wine, which was brought to him. It was sour on his tongue, hot in his throat, and set his mind afire.

After a few more sips, he beckoned Markí inside the litter and offered him the skin. The boy took it, drank, coughed, splashing the wine and his spittle onto the carpeted floor. Archibald did not mind.

*He drank it*, he thought, *and did not falter.* "Have you a last name, Markí?"

"I told you, I'm an orphan-"

"All in my kingdom must address me as, *Eminence*," Archibald said, pointedly. "It tempts my anger when I am not. Try again, boy."

"I told you, *Eminence*. I'm an orphan, *Eminence*. Maybe my papa was someone important, but my mother was a whore. She died when I came out of her. I was raised by others-"

"I've heard enough, Markí. A soldier with no last name is hardly a soldier at all-"

"But *you* invited *me*!" the orphan shouted. He stood, stooping because of the ceiling, and made to leave the litter. Archibald called him back.

"Markí, I sympathize with you. I shall call you, *Commons*."

The orphan pondered a moment. His mouth clenched, and his bottom lip trembled. Despite his strength and resilience, it was the second time the king saw tears spring to his eyes. "*Commons* names me for what I am: a common boy with common blood." Still, he did not leave the litter, only had his hand against the silk.

"And yet what commoner stares glory and honor in the eye? Your name shall be Commons, but I promise you your deeds shall be aught but."

Markí Commons moved away from the flowing curtains and sat again on the cushion opposite Archibald, who drank once more from the wineskin before passing it to the orphan. The wretch refused with a wave of his hand. "I don't like it."

"Tis strong, sooth. 'Twas meant for kings and lords. Nowhere else shall you find a better tiger bone wine than this."

"What is that?"

"Rice wine fermented with the corpse of a scimitiger. It is sour, I know, but potent and good for ailments. *Drink.*"

Again, the boy hesitated. "I like sweeter things."

"As do I. But in positions such as ours, we must learn to enjoy the finer tastes." He extended his arm and even shook the skin. The liquid sloshed from inside. "*Drink.*"

For the second time, the boy took the wineskin and put it to his lips. He pulled it from his lips, spitting and coughing. "It isn't any better than before!"

"Did you falter because you knew its bitterness now?"

Markí looked at him as though he might yell, or even attack. But the boy did not move.

"Yes," he answered. "That's why. But why does it concern you? I told you I didn't like it."

"Yes, you told me." Archibald raised the wineskin to his lips again, but a knock from outside the litter made him pull away. "Come!"

Da'Żern, red of skin and black of hair, appeared between the silken curtains. "I've returned. Gord is dead."

"I thought as much. Thank you, da'Żern. We may commence

the procession to Bugross."

But da'Żern did not move. Instead, he eyed the boy with an acerbic glare. "Eminence, Gord is dead by this one's stone."

"I'm *aware*, da'Żern," Archibald hissed through gritted teeth. "We may commence the procession to Bugross."

Still, da'żern did not move. *He begins to try my patience. Would Grandfather know to kill him?*

"I did not expect you to share your litter with one such as he—"

Archibald stood. "Should I not? You seem concerned with mine assessments. Sooth, the orphan stinks as a rankled wound. But he is now my soldier named Markí Commons. You'd be wise to remember that."

Da'Żern scowled. "Yes, Eminence. We—"

"And if *ever* you think to undermine mine orders again, I'll have you turn that sword upon yourself!"

Da'Żern's jaw clenched. "We shall away now."

Archibald smiled and returned to his seat. "Good. You'd best leave now, Markí."

The boy's eyes widened. "*Leave?*"

"Of course, for servants ride not in litters with their kings.

You've now a task to do. Your hand felled the porter. Your hand replaces his at the yolk."

The boy's face twisted. Before he could lash out, Archibald stopped him. "Remember, you're surrounded by *my* soldiers. One yelp from me and there shall be no more yelps from you."

The orphan paused, defeated.

"Steady your hips when rising and lowering," said da'Żern. He stepped aside to allow Markí to leave. The curtains flapped closed, created a small breeze that played on Archibald's face.

But he frowned once more. "Da'Żern."

The curtain opened again by the Forest Dancer's hand. "Yes?"

"Remind Markí Commons that I shall have a smooth ride else he shall not."

Da'Żern smiled. He had a flair for punishing those Archibald did not approve of. "As you command."

The King sat back on his cushions and sighed. "Damn, but it's hot."

A soldier outside called to three, and the litter rose, shakily. The train continued then, with bumps and jostles being rare. *It seems Commons has a good back as a porter. But that makes him a knight not. His true challenges are yet to come.* The King's smile lingered when the fetid stench was behind them, left burning on his memories.

They reached Bugross Bay in three days. The air smelled of sand, surf, and sweat.

Archibald shriveled his nose. *Disgusting.*

The squelch of grass soon turned into the squish of sand, and then heavy footfalls against wooden planks. Markí Commons had grown easier with the litter. The dismount was smooth, almost effortless. The baggage and supply trains were behind them still.

Archibald met a fat old man, bald of pate, with a thick, white side mustache that created a bridge from his ears over his upper lip. He smiled, revealing several missing teeth. Worn at his rotund waist was a thin, straight sword.

"Eminence, the pleasure is mine." He gestured over the horizon. The sky was as resplendent as the King, billowy and velvety, with purple, red, and gold. The setting sun, burning red, emblazoned the rolling seawaters. Reclining in the waters was a double-hulled junk with fanned sails of silver and a hull of rosewood. "You've come so close to nightfall, Eminence. Allow me the pleasure of alighting you in my quarters. You shall sail first thing on the morrow—"

Archibald eyed the ship, ignoring the Duke of Bugross. "No. We sail tonight."

Da'Żern shuffled. "Forgiveness, Eminence, but the men are

41

tired—"

Archibald snapped his head toward him. "*Are* they? They did not rest well as we camped?"

Again, da'Żern the Damned hesitated. "You were restless. We made camp at the coming of night, and then you roused us all but hours later, reminding us we are late—"

This was true. Archibald often remained alert at night, now more than ever. He hoped to hear from Father and Grandfather, but they no longer came. Even Rąd was gone from him. He started to wonder if he had been deserted, if they were disappointed in him.

*It is because I am late*, he told himself during the night. *If I hurry and make Stonehill, then they will again reveal themselves to me—they must*!

He poked da'Żern's mail. "I have warned you once never to question me. Need I warn you again?"

"No, Eminence."

"Good, because there *shan't* be a second warning." Archibald looked to the portly duke. "We sail tonight. I shan't have need for a litter then, and there shall be cabins aplenty for the men."

"Eminence, we cannot leave just yet."

"Da'Żern, you tread upon quickening sand—"

"I speak out not against you, but for Markí Commons." He aimed his hand at the boy. "He will need mail and a weapon. I shall train him as a Forest Dancer."

"A good thought. We shan't want the boy to come defenseless into Stonehill. However, I disagree with your tutelage."

Da'Żern gasped. "But—!"

Archibald sneered, appreciating the traitorous knight's floundering. "He'll instead be a water dancer, overseen by al'Foyl."

"Don't I get a say in anything?" the urchin asked.

Archibald directed his venomous gaze to him. "Not unless you want to keep your tongue." The boy quieted. "Take him, al'Foyl. Get him prepared. You know where we'll be."

Al'Foyl, a tall, gangly man with big knuckles and a high forehead, took the urchin by the arm. He led him over the wooden planks that made up the walkways. Archibald looked again to Duke Wobbegong.

"Show us now to *King's Glory*."

"Right this way, Eminence."

The fat old duke led them across the planks, over bridges made of stone, and finally onto the pier where the junk waited in still waters. The gangplank lowered, and seven people bearing the blue shark of House Wobbegong guarded it from the wharf. They bowed their heads when the King walked by.

Duke Wobbegong looked pleased with himself. "These are but a few of the sailors I shall have accompanying you on your voyage. There are enough supplies to last just over a moon if you are careful, giving you food enough for the return as well. Captain Welmá knows to stop at the Falawyspa Archipelago as well."

"Good. Da'Żern did well to request that."

"The pleasure was mine, Eminence."

"Of course it was, you milksop."

Archibald looked again to the *King's Glory*. The first sprinklings of stars dotted the sky, now dark as wine. *If we leave now, I may tonight see Grandfather.* "Let us be on it and on our way."

# 4: Áśwąg In The Archipelago

*King's Glory* pulled into dock ten days after her departure from Bugross Bay. The sea had been mostly calm, save for some storm clouds on the horizon. The captain outran them.

*Good*, Archibald thought when a servant told him. *My servants must know my needs before I ask them.*

Mostly Archibald remained confined to his quarters, but always with a servant nearby to answer his beck and call.

Being upon the ship was a tedious thing indeed, especially when Grandfather had yet to reappear. No matter how long he remained submersed in darkness, there was still no sign. It was beginning to become worrisome. He took little drink and even less food. He refused visitors, saying that the captain and crew should know their duties without his aid. He denied even a single candle's flame to lift the heavy gloom.

*But it was all for naught*, he told himself now, as he and his men prepared to dock.

They came to his door at some time—he did not know when, for

45

he had not seen the sun in days—and told him they neared the island of Spęèl in the Falawyspa Archipelago.

Upon leaving his quarters, the king was immediately assailed by the sun. He drew up his sable-lined cloak over his eyes. Swearing, he walked weakly toward his soldiers. "Da'Żern? Al'Foyl?"

"We are at your side," said da'Żern.

A strong arm gripped his elbow, leading him. "I'll lead you to the litter. Your eyes will better adjust in the dimness of its curtains."

"You do me a kindness, da'Żern. I'll not forget it."

"It is my pleasure to serve you—"

"Then I trust you'll remember that the next time you think to stay your hand."

Archibald let the silk of his litter fall into place, hiding him once again from the outside world. The litter was lifted and then tilted after only a few steps, coming down the gangplank and stepping onto Spęèl, the second-largest island of Falawyspa.

The archipelago contained a thousand islands, the largest being Ćeldní. Several of the islands were too small to be inhabited by even a single village. Other islands, though large and fertile enough, would force the inhabitants to share the land with blasting mountains.

Oftentimes, ambassadors came from Falawyspa. He frowned. *Would that I ruled the archipelago instead of the chieftains.*

They seemed a savage people to him, worshipping the ring of blasting mountains that were found on each island. Grandfather once told him that traitors would be shoved down into the blasting mountains, burning alive before they even found the bottom.

That thought pleased him. Perhaps he might even route out a traitor before their stay was over and make Spèèl's chief throw him into one of those fiery mounds. He imagined the skin turning black and flaking away as ash.

He sucked in a deep breath and thought, *Mine eyes should return to me.*

The King opened the silken curtain by an inch or two and stared out into the world beyond. Mostly, there was ocean. Small fishing vessels with one or two men in them skimmed over the calm waters. The people—their hair black or brown, their skin tanned and tough from sun and sea—called to each other, working together to bring their catches in. Archibald watched as one young man drove his spear into the shallows and came up with a long silver princefish, its tail flapping as it suffocated.

Closer to the shoreline, women, naked with golden breasts and nut-brown nipples, emerged holding nets of fat oysters and clams as wide as saucers. Hair black as jet streamed down their backs in long, wet sheets. Most of them scrambled for their sun-whitened clothes, but others waved to the soldiers in the

47

procession, hoping to distract them.

*But they won't. My men know the penalty for halting.*

In the distance swayed bórbakee trees, thin stalks of scaly yellow wood with wide green leaves eleven feet in length. The air was alive with fire, the smells of sweet meat cooked with fruit over burning stones. Combating that scent was another: the salt air from the sea.

Frowning still, Archibald released the silken curtain.

*I should not have worn velvet this day. 'Tis already too warm. Should the chieftain wish to feast us by fire, I know not if I'll survive.* Silently, he fingered the sable edge of his cloak. *Then again, I must keep up appearances. Certainly, my servants should have no trouble allowing me to retire earlier than planned should I come to need it.*

The litter came to a stop and was settled gently onto the ground. One of the soldiers held the silken curtain open and he stepped out of it and looked around the jungle clearing. Overhead, hidden by the canopies, birds, and monkeys let out their calls, trilling and howling.

It was beautiful here. Nothing but sand, plants, oceans. If only it weren't so damnably humid.

Archibald's eyes landed upon the chieftain, a wide man with bronze skin and matching coif of hair. His eyes were black, filled with pride, smiling even more than his lips. He wore no facial hair, and neither had he donned a tunic or robe, allowing his expansive chest, oiled and hairless, open to the breezes. His britches, however, were stark white, and upon his sausage-like fingers were golden rings with gems of different sizes, cuts, and colors.

He was surrounded by men thinner and taller than himself, each without shirts as well. Their puffy britches, however, were stained pink, and in their hands were strangely bladed swords, single-edged and flanged with a fork near the point. The hilts were made of wood, and the pommels were made in the likenesses of leviathan heads.

Even as Archibald eyed suspiciously, the fat little chieftain stepped in front of his gaze, still smiling jovially.

"Your Eminence, welcome to Spęèl of the Falawyspa Archipelago!" Then he frowned—at least with his mouth—and said, "Your Eminence came overdressed. It becomes rather hot here. Would you not mind—?"

"But I *do* mind, Chief—"

He flushed, and then bowed. "Mądo. Forgiveness for my rudeness. It is a delight to see you here. We all grieve the loss of your father."

Archibald quirked an eyebrow. "You are forgiven, but let it happen not again. As for Father: he is dead. There is naught more to discuss. Now he looks down upon us as our other ancestors do. His hold over the kingdom, however, is no longer.

49

In death, he possesses naught."

"Yes."

Archibald chuckled. Now the fat chieftain smiled with his mouth, but no longer with his eyes. *Good, he is unnerved.* Knowing that created a taste in his mouth sweeter than any Falawyspan roasts.

"*King's Glory* is docked. My soldiers are gathering provisions which might take the better part of the day, and they wish not to leave so early at night." He cocked his head to the side. "Feast we tonight?"

The fat chieftain smiled again, this time with both eyes and teeth. "Can you not smell the delicate flavors that waft through our air? As we speak, brimbleboar and drop-monks are roasting with fire-pines, starfruit, and dragonberries. Flayed starfish are frying in sauces. Milkfish and emperorfish are cooking on beds of lemon, salt, and oil. Plantains are soaking in coconut milk before we fry them with sweet water from sugarcane."

"Ah," said Archibald, uninterested. "Sounds a feast most wonderful."

"Does it not? Walk with me, please. There is much I wish to know about. Many questions are on my tongue, and I want not to disturb the meal with such concerns."

Archibald looked to the shirtless soldiers and frowned. "Will they accompany us?"

The chieftain's eyes flickered. "Yes. They are my personal guards this day."

"If you've personal guards, then I shall see to it mine accompany me."

The fat chieftain's eyes widened, surprised, panicked perhaps. "It is not that I mistrust you, I only—they must—"

"Follow you wherever you go?" Archibald suggested.

Smiling. "Yes, Eminence."

"Mine, as well. They protect me from enemies and from traitors in my midst. No doubt you've heard of the deaths by my command? Commoners and nobles alike, meeting their ends by my soldiers' blades?"

The fear returned. "Yes."

"Good. Then you'll know you've naught to fear unless I think you a foeman or traitor." He craned his neck behind him. "Come, da'Żern, al'Foyl, and Commons as well, I suppose."

The flickering in Mądo's eyes gave way to fear. "But I've only two—"

"Commons is al'Foyl's squire. 'Twould only be meet for him to accompany his master." Archibald clicked his teeth and looked the fat chieftain right in his dark eyes. "You fear me. You do not mean to attack me, do you? And answer carefully for da'Żern kills quickly, but not without leaving cuts all along the body."

Mądo gulped. "I am *not* a traitor. I merely want to protect myself. And you."

"*Me?*"

"Yes, from pirates. They have been roaming the seas of late. They often stop here between Fangaard and the Badlands. It is always good to have precaution when traveling outside of your homestead, is it not?"

"With that, I can agree. Do you see Commons, there?"

The fat, craven chieftain nodded.

"He was an orphan boy that attacked my litter a fortnight ago, killing one of its porters with a stone. He and his friends attempted to ambush my procession. Perhaps if I'd traveled with less pomp, that would not have happened. However, I am inclined to show no fear, even in the presence of turmoil."

"But—"

Archibald smiled venomously. "Yes, Mądo?"

"I've heard of your purging traitors. Why did you not see the boy killed? Why outfit him with spear-mail and a battle fork?"

"One thing to remember, Mądo, something my grandfather told me: *All* men are traitors. However, they should be allowed to live out their usefulness. I did not see the lad as an enemy or traitor. Mine enemies are the Tourm-men, and the traitors are those rats within mine own city. He was an urchin, hungry for food and more. So, I gave him a place in mine army. And how does he fair, al'Foyl?"

Al'Foyl nodded. "Well. He's not long been in my charge, yet he is naturally skilled and eager to learn."

"See, Mądo? I *know* when a traitor is in my midst. I know that your guardsmen are not here for pirates, but for me, should you decide that you *are* a traitor. For *traitors* decide that they are traitors. Not I."

At some point, Archibald had gripped the man's thick arm. His own fingers were thin claws. When he pulled away, a dark ring was around the chieftain's wrist. He drew his face away from Mądo's. He relished in sweat that beaded the man's brow, the uncertain glances, the speechlessness.

Archibald, on the other hand, smiled wide and even snorted a laugh. "Now, shall we have that walk?"

Soldiers in tow, Mądo led Archibald through the hutted village where the people shucked their shellfish and skinned jungle cats of their pelts. There was no road, but a worn path between which bloodred malphighiales and rainbow-hued orchids sprung up. There was another hut in which a man tended a variety of birds not native to Fangaard. Most people, whether in their huts or out of them, stopped to stare as the finely-dressing king walked with the fat and oiled chieftain, tailed by their very different

53

soldiers.

"Your father was a well-respected man in these parts. I don't believe he ever visited all five-hundred-and-thirty-two inhabited islands, though. But there is hardly any time for that, I think. I know he came to the largest five every few years. Mostly he summoned all five-hundred-and-thirty-two chieftains to Spire Black. How we ever fit in the great hall, I will never know!"

Archibald frowned at the chieftain's gut. "Nor I."

"It *is* good to see you, though," said Mądo, unaware of the slight. "You've never been to the Falawyspa Archipelago yourself, have you?"

"Never, although I've heard tales from Father and Grandfather—" he looked around the area "—and their tales have done no justice to the beauty." He looked back to the oiled craven. "Tell me, Mądo, are there any blasting mountains upon Spęèl?"

"The beautiful Cloud Mountain lies ahead in the distance." He waved gold-ringed fingers in its direction. It was covered in trees and rose higher than any other hill on the island. "It is so humid in that jungle that it nearly always rains. However, it is not a blasting mountain. At least, we've no records of it ever erupting."

"A pity." Archibald again grew bored. "Tell me, chieftain, did you request this walk to show me regular mountains and flowers? Of mountains, I know plenty in Kendala. And though our flowers are different, we've a variety on the mainland as well."

The chieftain did not answer but darted his eyes about.

*A sign most ill.* Archibald halted Mądo once more, blocking the pig-man's vision of all else but his visage. "I'll know the reason for this walk. I promise you, 'tis not as innocent as you'd have me think. I'd have it now."

"On—" The giant toad stammered, and Archibald raised both eyebrows. "On the contrary, Your Eminence, I mean only to catch up with you. The news of your father's passing was a terrible thing—and your elder brother only a few years before. How are *you* faring?"

Archibald frowned. "I? I fare well. The cost of the throne was one great, sooth. But the greater cost is that which comes after: Ruling, the decisions. But it is what I was born to do, it seems. For reasons unknown to me, the ancestors thought it better to seat me than mine elder brother."

"Yes, your ancestors. And tell me, how did your father die? We've only heard *of* his passing."

"My father died from poisoned wine. 'Twas perhaps done by one of the servants, perhaps someone looking to usurp the crown. I know that my brother was drowned. Whether these murders were of the same forces—different puppets dancing under the same master—I cannot know."

Mądo eyed him wearily. When he spoke, his voice was a fearful whisper. "Is there not talk of it being *your* hand that makes the puppets dance? After all, you survived them."

*So, this is the truth.* Brow furrowed, he admitted, "I've been accused, yes. 'Twas for that reason I've increased the castle's soldiers, as well as those in my personal guard. 'Tis also why I've begun routing out traitors. Never do I want their fate to befall me."

"Nor should you. Drowning and poison are terrible ways for a life to end. In both cases the effect is slow, watching the life drain slowly from the victim until they breathe no more."

He paused, building the courage to ask his next question. "Do you think that is what happened? Do you think the killer rejoiced in the act? Do you think he remained to watch your father and elder brother suffer and die?"

While he spoke, the fat chieftain licked his lips. His eyes darted about. Archibald could smell the fear as clearly as the meats or sea breeze. But there was something more—something accusatory about his words and demeanor—even if fear was prevalent over all else.

Regardless, Archibald maintained his breathing. His eyes never left the chieftain's face, and he did not gasp or smile or do aught else with his mouth. He was impassive as he said, "I imagine it would be hard to force a person to breathe water without being there. As for the poisoner, I cannot know if he remained to watch my father die. Were it me, I would've fled the castle as soon as I knew he had imbibed."

Archibald raised his eyebrows, his gaze never faltering. "But I remained, Mądo. I remained to mourn. I remained to collect the scattered pieces left to me—nay, to build a legacy worthy of the Hŭdáshī dynasty. Most of all I remained because *it was not me.*"

Forehead to forehead, Archibald could smell the fruit and sweet leaves on the fat chieftain's breath.

"Forgiveness, I beg again—"

"Accuse me again and you'll wish your Cloud Mountain was of the blasting sort—a burst and blaze would serve a far less gruesome death than what I can conceive for you. Of that be certain."

Archibald stepped away from the chieftain. Mądo's personal guard had their hands upon their ornate wooden hilts, but da'Żern and al'Foyl held their weapons, bearing down on Mądo's guardsmen.

The villagers around them stared in disbelief. One of them, a washerwoman, even dropped her bucket of water, the liquid now turning yellow soil into mud.

Archibald clapped his hands.   "Da'Żern, al'Foyl, Commons—leave them.  Have we all forgotten that we come as friends? We seek respite, not war." He aimed a shaking finger eastward. "There—in Tourm—is the war."

Then he turned back to the chieftain. "Mine apologies, Mądo. I suffer it ill when I'm accused, especially when I'm accused of kinslaying. Kindly call your men off, as I have called off mine."

Mądo snapped his fingers. His soldiers removed their hands from the hilts.

Da'Żern, al'Foyl, and Commons relaxed as well. *But 'tis clear they want blood.*

Archibald smiled pleasantly. "I know not if I've routed out the man that has slain my father and brother. However, I know I have routed out many other traitors besides. Perhaps one was among them? As for the puppet master, his existence remains ever a mystery to me."

"A pity that you know not if your father's killer was brought to justice. I hope that you do restore the fine Hŭdáshī name. Is that not why you war with Tourm?"

"Of course, it is. Two hundred years ago, Tourm captured the western banks of the Lachlan River, driving Kendala past Durwyn's Finger. I say they have no claim to Nin, that the land is still ours. We attempted to take it back and again were pushed away."

"As far as you know, they believe the war over."

"I am no fool, Mądo. They know the war remains. Their next move is to reclaim Tourm's Gate. But as soon as I procure Stonehill's navy, my soldiers will again claim Tourm's Gate *and* march through the Sea of Trees."

Archibald cackled. A pity that Mądo did not share his laughter; a Kendalan victory meant a Falawyspa victory.

When Archibald's laughter faded, Mądo offered a wan smile. "You have it all planned out, then."

"Great victory oft comes with great planning."

"And you promise that you will not take men from Spęèl, Ćeldní, or any other island of Falawyspa? After all, we have no armies."

"Men may come if they wish for glory in battle. But no. I have no need of them. Does that settle your mind? Were you worried about maintaining the archipelago's peace?"

"The pirates are enough as it is, Your Eminence."

"Excellent." Archibald clapped his hands together. "The sun slowly sets, and my furs grow heavy. Where will the feast be held?"

The fat chieftain regained his nerves. He smiled with both mouth and eyes, which made his face appear to be melting, and led Archibald through more flora. Tall, vase-shaped flowers with tongues of blue and purple; plants low to the ground with many needle-thin teeth; trees with hanging vines and ruby red fruit.

Mądo took Archibald and his three guardsmen to a clearing. A clay house with a thatched roof lay in the center, near a stream of clear water popping with golden fish. Washerwomen gathered water, and cooks stood in front of wide grills, upon which animals lay motionless and unfeeling to the flames dancing beneath them.

Mądo grinned. "Don't they look delicious?"

On one grill, several small boars lined up, roasting. Upon another, at least two dozen skinned drop-monks lay in fetal positions with their tails curled around their bodies. An attentive cook spooned white gravy over them, making the fires plume happily. The flaky, white milkfish, and golden, fatty emperorfish, each lay upon glowing coals, surrounded by a strange assortment of fruits and vegetables.

Archibald eyed them all contemptuously, wrinkling his nose. "Indeed, they do. So, you expect your king to have his meal from the griddle?"

"No, Your Eminence. We dine in my garden, underneath canopies of leaves and silk."

Throughout the clay hut, several servants, all women, some with the same golden skin and straight black hair that he had seen diving for oysters, and others short and stocky, with big eyes, hair that came around their heads like clouds, and skin the color of raw clay. Mostly they cleaned, though some watered the many plants that decorated the spacious hut. One was even deciding which silken rope the chieftain would wear this evening.

"Your servants do you a service," Archibald said. "'Tis rare that one finds those who think in their master's stead. It is what all servants should strive for."

Mądo smiled at the compliment. "Thank you. Your words are kindness."

They exited the hut and wandered through the gardens behind it. *It looks just as it did when we were on the road here—however this time there is no road.*

Flowers, many of the same variety that they saw, grew from the ground and hung from the drooping branches of trees. Another difference that Archibald noticed was that there were no villagers—only servants that tended to the plants and the animals.

A silvery needle snake twisted its way down a branch no wider than a finger, and a majestic monkey-eating eagle, with lavender tail feathers and silvery, puffed head, sat regally upon a boulder.

Toward the back of the garden, the festivities were being attended by servant girls wearing colorful but shapeless dresses of dyed hemp. They set bowls and dishes onto the rows of long, wooden tables. As promised, the lords' table was sheltered under a canopy of bright pink silk, studded with tiny crystals glistening in the twilight.

Mądo sat beside the King, smiling wide. "It is hours still until the other guests arrive, but I wonder if I might tempt my king with some wine."

61

"Other guests?"

"A dozen other chieftains come tonight. We are all so curious of Kendala's affairs. Lords come as well, landowners and farmers and fishermen. Merchants, all."

"Good." He frowned. "To fill this fine garden with ill rabble would be a slight against me. Oft do I wonder of Falawyspa. My father enjoyed it here—as did my grandfather. I begin to see why. Perhaps when I've conquered Tourm, I'll parade the Unbreakable's head around all five-hundred islands."

"Ahem—about the wine?"

Archibald waved him off. "Commons, bring the tiger bone wine. The finest wine in all of Kendala, better surely than your jungle swill."

Mądo swallowed hard but said not a word. Like the bowls and plates, the cups were small and wooden. Commons poured tiger bone wine for each of them, careful not to spill. Archibald had not told him, but it was good to know he knew not to regardless.

Each of the men raised their cups.

"To Kendala!" Archibald bellowed.

Mądo's replied less fervently. "Kendala."

They drank together, each finishing the entire cup before replacing them on the table. Archibald smiled. It was sour to the point of rancidness, and it burned all the way down his gullet. Still, it was smoother than the clearest water.

Mądo looked less enthralled. *But at least he drank.*

"I fear I shall never be used to the taste."

"It is one acquired. I would know. But I had a taste before bed since I was six-and-ten. I've grown to enjoy it more with each passing summer."

"Yes, well, we do not ferment 'tiger corpses on these islands for there are none. Mayhap—"

"'Tis all I wish to drink, and it is quite rude not to drink with your king. Now, more, Commons, for both of us."

The lad again filled each wood cup with the cloudy liquid. Again, each man drained the wine, and Archibald promptly demanded more. By nightfall, the guests had arrived, and the bronze chieftain wavered with a fevered glow about his face. Archibald, however, sat without hindrance from the liquor. He did not feel sluggish or flush, and he did not believe his cheeks accumulated any color.

The lords' table soon filled with a dozen other chieftains from a dozen other islands, none of which Archibald cared to know the names of.

The food was served. First came the clams and oysters, raw with a sweet onion sauce. After that was the white milkfish and

63

golden emperorfish, succulent and bold of flavor, not nearly as spicy as he thought they would be. The third course was the brimbleboar and drop-monks. In the end, the hands and faces of nobles and soldiers alike shined with grease. They were encouraged to pull the meat from the 'boars' faces and suck their feet clean. The drop-monks were no different: Mądo said the tastiest parts were the eyes and brains, which were stewed and spiced before being served.

The guests drank sweet, pink flowerwine, but Archibald made certain he had enough flasks of tiger bone wine to last throughout the meal. Servants took the skeletal remains of pig and monkey away and brought out fried plantains soaked in coconut milk, and plenty of fresh fruit if one desired something lighter.

But Archibald felt flush. He felt *hot*. Regret now for wearing the sable-lined cloak. His breathing changed. The night air was cooler but no less humid. Sweat dripped down his sallow cheeks, and his hair felt wet and heavy upon his head.

One of the chieftains turned to ask him something, but he stood abruptly. The chatter around the table ceased, and Mądo eyed him.

"I've become too hot. Too much wine and sun. I cannot remain here. I must retire."

Mądo gasped. "A terrible thing. Shall I have one of the girls show you to your quarters?"

"Please," he said, struggling to breathe. "Da'Żern, al'Foyl,

Commons, to me."

The dancers stood, but Markí Commons dug his fork into his plantain. Al'Foyl gripped his shoulder. With a voice like falling gravel, he said, "Up, you. You're finished." The lad did not argue.

One of the dark-red serving girls, dress bright green, appeared. "Take him to his quarters, please. Our king needs rest."

Silently, she nodded and led the four through the gardens and into the clay hut. She found the king's room. It had no door, but instead, shoots of wood were tied to the threshold and swung from strings of braided drop-monk hair.

Archibald waved the serving girl away and entered the room. Certainly, his soldiers would remain vigilant outside. The room was plain, the bed wide and square and inviting. Its cushions were silken, stuffed with softness.

He summoned da'Żern. "Aid my undressing."

"We were discussing our watches," said da'Żern as he removed the heavy cape. Immediately the world became cooler.

"Tell me, da'Żern, do you believe we are safe here?"

"Why, Eminence? Did Mądo say something?"

"A feeling I have. If only Grandfather could appear. He would best know how to discern mine unease."

65

Da'Żern said nothing but continued to remove Archibald's boots. After that was his black velvet doublet, and then the sweat-stained tunic he wore underneath.

"We'll remain by your doorway and your bedside if you command it of us. We shan't let any harm—or even the fear of harm—disturb your sleep."

*The fool knows not what he says.* "Leave me, da'Żern."

As his soldiers waited outside the room—or perhaps even rejoined the festivities—Archibald blew out the candle and crawled beneath the cushions, softer even than clouds.

Try as he might, he found no surcease.

Eyes shut, head buried in silk, he whispered again and again, "Where are you, Grandfather?" The sounds from the jungles and the laughter from the feast rang in his ears like a sword dropped in an empty armory.

"Where—?"

No matter how soft the pillows were, it was still terribly hot. So hot, he felt buried.

*This place shall be the death of me.*

Unless he moved.

He threw off the cushions. The night air sweltered. His eyes

66

were wide and as dry as the rest of him. He gripped the cushions and could not think. He tried to gasp for air, but smoke trailed from his mouth.

Up he came, and off the bed. He peeked out from behind the clattering wooden shoots. Neither da'Żern nor al'Foyl were present, and Commons leaned against the wall, snoring.

*The churl.*

But it mattered not. *I need to sleep. I need to dream. I need to see Grandfather. But it's too hot*!

He wandered out into the night, aimless, touching houses, scrambling through bushes—and then there was a weight on his shoulder.

He turned around, eyes wide.

"Grandfather?"

"No," breathed the gaunt stranger, thinner even than Archibald. The five teeth he had were yellow or brown, soon no longer for the haven of his mouth. "What is it you seek?"

"My grandfather."

"You seem a little old to worry for your grandfather."

"He is dead, but I need to *see* him."

The stranger pushed his blackened tongue between two broken teeth. Finally, he said, "I can show you him."

"You can?"

"For a price."

"Name it."

"One golden szirvl."

"Of those I have none. But I can give you a gold tiger's head instead."

"Kendalan money, and a thicker coin besides. Come with me and tell me more."

Archibald, coated in sweat, followed the stranger through the rushes. "Grandfather comes to me in dreams, tells me who to trust, finds traitors for me. He has been gone from me. Mine elder brother keeps him from my mind. If I am to win the war against Tourm, I need him."

"You'll see him. First, the coin."

Archibald did not mind that the stranger spoke to him so casually. He withdrew a tiger's-head coin, glistening in the moonlight. He handed it to the stranger, who returned the kindness by plucking something from the ground.

When Archibald took it, it was soft and satiny in his fingers, but also oily.

"Think of your grandfather and eat that mushroom. You'll see him soon enough." Cackling, the stranger left Archibald where he stood.

It did not matter that he paid a tiger's head for something growing on the ground. He was lost, and he needed aid.

"I know not my way back."

But the stranger was gone.

Dismayed, Archibald looked to the small mushroom in the center of his palm, a purple cap with a black, feathery rim. His grandfather's wrinkled old face came to his mind, smiling proudly. Archibald put the mushroom on his tongue and thought. *Now if only Rąd interferes not.*

He began to chew. Juice from the tiny mushroom gushed with each bite. He closed his eyes. *That damnable Rąd shall interfere no longer. Grandfather will help me see—no!*

Gradually, Rąd's face overtook his grandfather's until it was the only one in the blackness behind his eyelids. His elder brother wore a haughty look, a look that meant Archibald had failed.

Archibald panicked, but logic soon crept in. *This is not* real! But when he opened his eyes, Rąd had not vanished. He remained standing amidst the malphighiales and purple, feathery mushrooms.

"*No!*"

*You fool, did you think I was done with you?  Now you are surrounded by your enemies. Mądo wishes nothing more than to see you dead.*

Archibald stepped backward. "Why?"

The smirk deepened. *He fears for his island. He fears for his people. He wants you dead because you're dangerous. It has nothing to do with the war. It is him or you.*

"No!"

Archibald ran through the woods, not knowing where he was going but seeking shelter somewhere.

*Why do you run? You go the wrong way. Continue, and you only go to your death.*

"No!  Leave me be!  Where is Grandfather!  I wish to see Grandfather!"

*Continue, and you shall.*

Archibald stumbled from the jungle and onto a rush-lined path. Houses of baked clay with thatched roofs. Back in the village. His eyes were wide; he did not think he could blink even if he wanted to.

Outside of the large house in a clearing were two men.

Archibald's eyes widened even further when he saw them. One was tall, muscular, with a stooped back and black hair that hung over his face. The other was a fat man with a jowly chin and beady black eyes.

*Orrick the Unbreakable and Castellan ka'Vín, outside the chieftain's hut! He was mine enemy! Mądo summoned them here to kill me!*

The two spotted him. They each held swords, the same flanged blades with the wooden dragon hilts native to these islands.

Archibald searched the ground. He found a large stone and hefted it. *I shall mimic Commons.* Then he looked to Orrick and ka'Vín.

"Your Eminence?" said Orrick. "Please put the stone down. Come with us. We'll return you to your room—"

"Belittle me not with words titles false! Following you shall lead me only to the void! You go, and I *shan't* follow!"

"What—?"

Archibald hurled the stone and smashed Orrick's face. The hot night air became crisp with the sound of crunching bone.

Ka'Vín drew his sword, but Archibald hefted Orrick's and impaled the turncloak through the middle of his stomach, releasing his bowels. "'Twas foolish of you to come unarmored!" He drew the flanged edge from his body and slashed through ka'Vín.

71

Panicked, Archibald looked toward the hut. No one had seen him kill Orrick and ka'Vín, but that did not mean others weren't looking for him.

*Mądo is a traitor. Rąd spoke true. He means to kill me. I shall return the favor!*

Archibald continued through the red clay hut. The griddles now lifeless. The meal was done. He wandered through the house and was approached by one of the servants: a pale girl with chestnut hair and a pockmarked face. Her breasts bounced as she approached, naked to the humid night.

*The Ninnish whore is here, too!*

"Eminence, why are you out of bed?" Her eyes widened as he drew himself into the moonlight through the windows. "Your eyes are bloodred! And why do you hold a bloody *Kąpiłą?*"

That should not matter to the Ninnish slut. Whatever evil tricks Mądo played were illegal. Black magic, necromancy, was the work of devils. The thought made Archibald scowl. "You are supposed to be dead!"

She opened her mouth to scream, he slashed her throat before the sound was realized. Then he took her head, so she could return no more.

Covered in the blood, Archibald moved to the back of the hut and out into the beautiful garden. Flowers that were merely bulbs in the daytime had opened to sprawling petals, blue and purple and luminescent so that roaring bonfires were unnecessary.

Archibald made his way to the lords' table and found da'Żern, al'Foyl, and Commons sitting near the Spęèlo Chief. All looked concerned, but da'Żern approached him.

"Eminence, how worried we were! I'd gone to relieve Commons of his duties. He had fallen asleep. You weren't in the hut, and we sent soldiers to find you—"

"And find you they *did*." Mądo stood up, scowling. "That's a Kąpiłą! No doubt you wear my guardsmen's blood. Is this how you repay my hospitality?!"

"Your guardsmen." He aimed the sword at Mądo, causing guardsmen to draw their own swords. "You welcomed me with hospitality false! The guardsmen you sent were Orrick the Unbreakable and Castallen ka'Vín. You mean to see me dead!"

"What madness has possessed you?"

"To make matters worse, I was confronted by a Ninnish slut that I killed over a moon past." He swung the sword. "Dealings with devils are punishable by death, Mądo!"

"My serving girl?" He looked about. "Guards, detain him! But do not hurt him! His eyes are red and unblinking! This is not Archibald but an Áśwąg! Capture it and make him tell us where he has hidden our king!"

Archibald pointed his sword at the chieftain. "Kill him,

da'Żern!"

Da'Żern hesitated, damn him, and looked to the chieftain. "Áświg?"

"A shape-shifting devil! He has stolen our king and has taken his form! He must be detained but unharmed so we might find our true king!"

"I *am* the true king! Now kill him, da'Żern! Kill them all!"

"He is not an Áświg," said da'Żern, "but neither is he our king. Something happened to him. He is prone to fits such as these, but never with such intensity. We shall detain him, but interrogation is unnecessary. Please, Your Eminence, lay down your sword—"

"Never! I've always despised how you hesitate when I command you! If you're too craven to kill them, I'm not!"

The guests—traitors, all—gasped as Archibald leaped up and jumped over the table with strength not his own. Before Mądo could move, before his guards could react, Archibald jammed the kąpiłą into Mądo's fat neck. Blood sprayed out as yellow fat rolled out from the wound. His eyes bugged out as he choked on his own humors. Screams ensued from the guests, who scrambled from the garden as more bare-chested guardsmen poured in.

Archibald yanked the blade from the chieftain's neck and lashed out against a guardsman. He leaped away, but another was soon upon him, shouting, "Kill the Áświąg!"

He defended, but the first attacker returned. Da'Żern's blade spun like a whirlwind. Al'Foyl danced away from a thrust, lunged, and impaled the guardsman through his bare chest, spilling blood everywhere. Two other warriors fell upon them.

"Commons!" shouted al'Foyl. "Get His Eminence back to *King's Glory*!"

Markí approached, crying, "No!"

Commons lunged and Archibald struck out, but Commons caught the blade with his battle fork. He twisted and the blade came free from his grip.

"Traitor!" screamed Archibald, but Commons struck his temple with the butt of his spear. He nearly toppled but Commons grabbed him and hoisted him up.

"Sorry, but I gotta take you to safety."

Behind him, the fires roared. Kąpiłą rang out against da'Żern's cicada wing and al'Foyl's battle fork.

As Commons led him through the jungle, cries of "Áświąg!" rose higher than Cloud Mountain.

# 5: The False Emperor

The lurching sea did naught for Archibald's pounding head. He demanded tiger bone wine. He demanded food. He demanded more light, then less light, then utter darkness. But there was naught he could do to quell the sea's churning.

*I will die like this*, he thought. *What did I do? I do not remember.*

That last thing he knew was waking with a start.

The nightmare was a new one.

His brother had come to him, killing him over and over again. Each time a different death.

Rąd held King Archibald's head under the shallows.

Rąd told da'Żern to pierce his heart.

Rąd told Commons to smash his head in with a rock.

Rąd commanded da'Żern to cleave his face.

*How dare he command the King's men! He is not the King! He is dead!*

That was the truth. He knew it was truth.

Still, the nightmare would not pass.

It was a nightmare that he struggled with for days.

Finally, he woke up covered in sweat. He opened the door and fell onto the deck. The sun beat down overhead. The light was pure whiteness. Still, he could not shield his eyes.

*I must keep them open. My brother hides in the void of my mind!*

But his servants were there. Not Orrick, ha'Qíj, not ka'Vín, but Commons, and he looked concerned.

He aided him up and gave him water. Commons even cut him small bites of food. Archibald's teeth felt shattered, his tongue felt swollen. He swallowed the morsels without chewing or tasting.

Commons told him to drink slowly. At first, he refused. *"No one commands a king!"* But when he retched, he heeded the advice.

Even after waking, the rolling sea beat against his skull. In the dismal candlelight, he kept his eyes clamped so tight they watered. When he ventured a look, he saw his hands were covered in blood. He closed his eyes again as the cooling water dribbled down his skin. He was being washed.

"What happened?" he said through clamped teeth. His entire face felt clenched. It even hurt to speak.

There was silence. *Hesitation.* And that he liked not at all. "Tell me."

"Something possessed you," said da'Żern. "You claimed to see Orrick and ka'Vín. I know not how, but you escaped from your bed. When you returned to the feast, you opened Mądo's throat."

"And then?"

Another blasted pause. He could have sworn the Forest Dancer was conspiring with another, but Archibald was blind to it.

"You fell unconscious. We fought many of the island's men. We were outnumbered, but greater skilled. We brought you back to *King's Glory* and made her sail. They don't pursue, but no longer do I believe they can be counted as allies. If we need supplies, we must forego the archipelago. No doubt word has spread to all five-hundred and forty-two islands."

Archibald pondered. Something within the tombs of his mind told him that he sought relief, and then naught.

*That is not true. There was something more: horror.*

He did not remember what he was afraid of, but he remembered the terror. He remembered the feeling that everyone on that barren island was out to kill him. Perhaps he was not wrong.

*All I know is what my men tell me. And all men are traitors.*

A knock drew his attention. But the darkness black as pitch, he questioned the action's validity. "Come!" he demanded. The door creaked. He recoiled. A sliver of light—hotter than any blasting mountain—scorched his face.

"How are you resting?"

"Da'Żern, you trouble yourself too much with me."

"No, it is my plea—"

"Again," snarled Archibald. "Again, you misread me! I was commending you *not*. I was telling you that you're too concerned with me. I have been commanded by many people—you included—to rest. And how might I do so with your constant interruptions?"

"Apologies, Your Eminence. You are correct. But I came with news."

"Speak it. Then *leave*."

"We near Stonehill."

Archibald smiled. There was naught he could do to help it.

"If the wind keeps up, we shall be there by dusk."

There was a dip in the light, no doubt da'Żern bowing. The door closed with a soft click. Archibald's eyes popped open, no longer hindered by the light.

"Damnable thing! How shall I ever meet with Emperor Bosker if I cannot face the light? I've no choice. I *must* face the light, pain though it brings me."

He threw his legs over the bedside. The entire ship seemed to move with him, lurching. *Kill it.* He clenched his teeth and continued. Legs threatening to give out under him, he balanced himself with the nightstand, knocking over a pitcher of warm wine.

After the clatter, which bit his brain like a beast, Archibald stood and moved to the door. He fell once but stood and continued. *If I were a god, this sea would have rocked its last.*

His hands found wood. Then, cold iron. He opened the door only a crack. The sliver of light was as pale as the moon but brighter than the sun.

Slender fingers pried the crack wider. He expected his skin to boil and melt from his hands. But the sensation never came. He peered into the hallway. Small candles flickered, dripping wax into their lamps.

"It is not so bright."

He stepped out into the hall and looked around, eyes squinting. His hand felt the wooden planks of the walls. His legs carried him, wobbly. But he had done it. He had left his infernal quarters and now walked the halls. Whatever light had plagued him moments ago had faded.

*What if it was no light? What if it was—?*

Grandfather's wise eyes, his kind smile, white hair as eternal as the clouds.

*I was looking for him.*

Archibald recoiled in horror. He remembered now how his brother came to him, speaking of Mądo's falsehood. He taunted him. *But that taunt was a warning, one that I did not take lightly.*

"What have I done?"

*Precisely as you should have.*

Archibald spun around. In robes of sky and sun, his grandfather stood before him. His hair and long beard wafted in an invisible breeze, one that Archibald could not feel. His eyes were just as wise, his mouth just as kind.

"Grandfather! I thought my brother beset you! I thought you lost to me!"

*Why would you think that?*

"Because—" Archibald's voice fell to a whisper "—you weren't come in so long."

*A test. I needed to make certain you were prepared for what Stonehill brings.*

"I know what they bring: a navy, and certainty in Tourm's defeated."

*Do you not remember? It should have been fortified in your mind after the incident in the archipelago.*

"All men are traitors."

*Even Emperor Bosker Reign. However—*

"That does not mean he shouldn't outlive his usefulness." Archibald pondered.

*I know what you think.*

"And?"

"Your Eminence!" Da'Żern stood before him, green silken cape rippling with each step. He held the cicada wing.

"Dammit, da'Żern why do you disturb me when I'm with my—" But Grandfather was gone. He exhaled. "Never mind. Why are you come?"

"We dock soon. I came to tell you. Why are you out of bed?"

"I could not in so sickly a state meet the Holy Lands' Emperor."

"You now feel well?"

"Better than before, yes. And I remember all." His brow furrowed. "But they were traitors, I promise you. Elsewise they shan't have met their demise."

Archibald turned to his cabin door. "I prepare now to disembark. Send a steward to dress me. And of Commons."

"Commons, Eminence?"

"He hit me with the butt of his battle fork. While he damaged me, he did so to save my life." He offered da'Żern a haunted smile. "He was good to do that. He must not be killed—but certainly punished."

"If you will allow me a suggestion, can it wait for our voyage home?"

"Your notion is wise, da'Żern. We do not wish to appear sniveling in front of Stonehill. His punishment will wait. Now fetch my steward."

Archibald dressed in the finery of his realm: A coat of maroon silk with gold-cloth along the hems of the garment. Britches of black were upon his legs, and leather shoes with pointed toes on his feet. His black hair was dipped in flowery oil and slicked back.

He found his way to the deck just as *King's Glory* was docking. A small town was built along the coastline. Houses of gray stones and mortar. Some roofs were thatched, but most were clay tiles. Beyond the town were forests and rivers that led to the sea. A large mountain range was behind all that, some of the peaks disappeared beyond the clouds, and most of their bases were fatter than the entirety of Zachwalaç.

But those mattered not at all. Around *King's Glory*, and even in the water away from the coast, were longships with curved prows and figures in the shapes of different beasts. It was enough to make Archibald giddy. *There must be nearly a gross!*

Da'Żern, al'Foyl, and Commons—as well as the other soldiers he took with him—bowed.

"Be on your guard," he told his men. "We come as friends. I know not what shall happen if we're not greeted as such."

The gangplank lowered and the procession disembarked. Upon the wharf were two people. A woman with golden skin stood straight as a spear. Her nose was overlong and pointed. Her eyes small and watery. Her tawny hair was constricted into a tight bun.

Beside her was a tall man in a breastplate of burnished bronze. The same material guarded his knees and shins, elbows, and forearms. He wore a blue chiton underneath. His head was covered in a half-helm, the tail feathers of a seahawk sprouting from the center and trailing down. At his side was a curved shortsword.

"Who've we here?" asked Archibald. "Surely not the emperor

and his wife?"

"No," said the woman, voice curt and nasally. "I am Ribée Clágr, Chancellor of Stonehill. Beside me is Lord Captain of the Shoreguard, Grág Enoź. And you are Archibald the Second Hŭdáshī, the Young Tiger, King of Kendala?"

"The very same." Archibald looked at them. "Why is Emperor Bosker not here to greet me?"

"The Emperor always sends delegates to meet with foreign dignitaries. Please do not take it as a slight. It is Stonehill custom."

"A shameful one," said Archibald. "I've always met with my visitors."

"As I said, it is no slight. We were asked to take you to Stone-cephar."

She moved aside and Archibald was taken aback.

Before the Kendalans' eyes were two dragons, each twenty feet long. Their hides were brown and scaly, their tongues sharp and curious as they licked the air. They were leashed to a gilt carriage, spikes protruding from the wheels.

"Skałagads," said Ribée. "Mobile dragons that we use for transportation." A small smile brightened her face. "The name means—"

"*Stone Lizard* in the Holy Tongue," said Archibald. "I am aware."

Ribée raised her eyebrows, impressed. "You are learned of the Holy Tongue?"

"All highborn Kendalans are."

"One thing you might not have known about the skałagads: they are the emblem of House Reign. Do you see the flags?"

"I do." They were like House Hŭdáshī's banners. The skałagad was burnished bronze, longwise on a field of turquoise. The banner was edged in gold-cloth. "A joyous pairing, it seems, skałagads and scimitigers."

Ribée smiled once more, and Grág guffawed and said, "Come with us, Your Eminence. We shall take the skałagads to Stone-cephar Palace."

"The carriage seats only four," said the Chancellor.

"I and Lady Ribée shall accompany you, along with one from your guard. We've more wains in which the others of your precession shall ride in. Emperor Bosker shall meet you once all in your host are come."

"Tarry not. Our time at sea was most exhausting."

"No doubt you'll find all the comforts you require within Stone-cephar's halls. But we must first reach it."

86

"Da'Żern will remain by my side."

"You've made your selection. Grág?"

Grág led them all to the gilt carriage. The skałagads whipped their long tails. Their long tongues darted from their mouths. They seemed not to notice or care when Grág opened the doors and bade the three inside.

The inside was spacious, laden with jewel-colored pillows. Archibald reclined into them. He did not even mind that Da'Żern grew comfortable too.

*But not too comfortable. I shan't forfeit my life because he has become lazy as a fatted sow.*

The captain called, "We're ready, Gäph!"

The coachman cracked the reins, and the carriage began to move. The skałagads moved by whipping their tails back and forth, their backs slithering though their legs were strong enough to carry a load such as theirs.

*It is shaky, but at least the pillows provide ample cushion.*

"We think you'll appreciate all our realm has to offer," said Ribée. Her dour expression returned. "Because we've many of your host to bring with us, we shan't linger. But we shall point out certain landmarks along the way."

"If you wish," said the King. He did not mind the lesson.

87

However, he doubted he would take away much. *Stonehill and Kendala shall be allies and little more.*

There was a sudden crunch. The carriage tilted and the mobile dragons began climbing the rock face. Archibald gripped the pillows. His stomach felt as though it was pressed against his spine. His teeth clenched and his eyes narrowed. Da'Żern fared not at all better. His eyes darted, seeking an attacker. Ribée and Grág, however, remained calm. The captain even wore a smile on his face.

"Where do you take us?" Archibald asked.

"Stonecephar," said Grág. "The city proper lies at the mountain's base. The castle, however—"

"Be not unnerved," said Ribée. "This is merely the way of things. Mayhap a warning might have been given beforehand—"

"*Mayhap?*" snapped Archibald. His face contorted with words to shout. But he stoppered them and reclined again, trying to relax as his hosts did. *I cannot have da'Żern kill the chancellor and captain. Then I'd never have my navy.* "Yes, a warning would have done."

The Stonehillers exchanged glances.

"Look out the window," said Ribée. "See the sights of Stonehill as we near her highest peak!"

Scowling, Archibald did so. A snaking river cut through the

plains and fields. Eastward was a grand forest that covered a portion of the mountain range. The forest was green and shining and seemed even to grow out into the shallows of the ocean. A large, crescent-shaped lake was in the thick of it.

"Wosylas," said Ribée, "the Free Forest. Tribes of wood elves dwell within."

"One tribe," Grág huffed. "And they've ravaged the Sandlakes farmlands not a sennight past. Quite thoroughly, I might add."

"And the reason?" asked da'Żern. "Forgiveness if I ask out of turn, Your Eminence. 'Tis your safety concerns me most."

"Very well, Da'Żern."

"There is no need for worriment," said Grág. "The wood elves receive their magic by the forest and the moonlight. They attack only the small villages nearest the edge of Wosylas. Neither the city nor the castle of Stonecephar has ever suffered from them."

"Not yet, you mean." Archibald soured. "We've elves in Kendala as well, in a hinterland called Jasnylas. If we do not bother them, they shan't bother us. And light elves are considerably less savage than the wooden ones you've here."

"Then it is no wonder they've maintained a peaceful pact within your borders," Ribée said. "Then again, should they decide to break that pact, Kendala would certainly be doomed."

"And yet I don't believe they would. As I said, Chancellor, they are less savage than their cousins. And I am not so certain we would not be aware of their treachery. Forests burn and even with their elven magic, fire cannot be crushed."

"A point goodly made." Ribée smiled again, but only for a moment.

From their vantage point, they could see the entire expanse of Stonehill. Most of it was a mountainous, or at least hilly. The Free Forest to the east was small compared to the desert of the west. White remains glistened under the sun, peeking out from the yellow sands. The Boneyard, they called it. After that, there was only white foam and green sea.

When the mobile dragons pulled into a cave, Archibald was flaccid with boredom. However, the cavern's interior soon lifted his spirits. The floor was tiled with blue-veined marble. The ceiling overhead peaked in the center and was encrusted with mirrored gold. Purple tapestries draped from the walls, and chains swinging overhead lit the place from above.

"Welcome, King Archibald of Kendala, to Stonecephar Palace," said Ribée, beaming.

*A first time for aught.* But Archibald would be a fool not to realize the grandiosity of the palace. *The artwork, the architecture, that it is inside a mountain—*

"It puts Spire Black to shame!" awed Archibald.

A new voice joined them. "I'm happy to see you so enthralled at our demesne." It was a man, young, and only his shadow flickered in the golden light at the end of a corridor.

Ribée and Grág dropped to their knees and averted their eyes. "Your Majesty."

"Rise, please. Grág, your armor must be uncomfortable. And Ribée, you'll ruin your gown, expensive thing it is." The figure stepped from the shadows.

Tall, fit, and fain, he was a man a head taller and perhaps a hundred pounds heavier than Archibald, though his weight came from muscle. His skin was golden brown, his hair the color of sunberries, and his eyes blue as the crescent lake in the Free Forest. His chin was strong, his cheeks high, his smile straight and white.

"Welcome indeed!" The man dipped his head. "I am Emperor Bosker Reign, Sovereign of Stonehill, Emperor of the Holy Lands." He smiled again. "Well, most of it."

Archibald remained scowling. "I see there is no need for introductions. Your realm is smaller than Kendala, and at the mention of *most of it*, I wonder if you speak of the Free Forest?"

Bosker barked a laugh. "No, no. I see Ribée enticed you with current affairs. But it appears she left you in the dark to our history. The Holy Lands contain four separate regions. The continent is shaped as a cross, with Overseer Mountain being center. Its range covers all the realms. We are in the southeast. To the northwest is the snowy kingdom of Deluga. To the southwest is the nation of Flamberg. Argineld is in the northeast, which is *not* under our jurisdiction."

The Emperor paused for a moment. His smile faltered. "Then again, neither are Flamberg and Deluga. When mine ancestors claimed the other two realms, Argineld was next. Our tomes are blank concerning the following battle. Stonehill was pushed back, and the way was blocked."

Archibald raised his eyebrows. "The way?"

"Mine ancestors used some way to get their soldiers through the mountains. Though it expands through each realm, climbing them is unfeasible. Countless men would be lost on the journey. Instead, we believe there was a path or passage that was shut. Even my most aged historians cannot recount where it once was."

"What of sea travel?"

"Flamberg is surrounded by high cliffs, making docking impossible. Deluga is guarded by the galawhale. And no one knows the way to Argineld. The ships we've sent were all destroyed. How, I cannot tell you."

"So, you are emperor only in name?" Archibald frowned, disappointed. "Tell me, do the other realms know you claim to be their ruler?"

The false emperor's eyes shone. "I cannot know what their children are taught. Nor can I know their states of affairs."

*Yes, and we cannot have any more harm come to your galleys.* "As long as your neighboring nations do not pose a threat or attempt rebellion, I'm certain no harm will be done."

"Words true and wise." The false emperor looked around as if noticing something for the first time. "I do not mean to keep you within my gatehouse. Please, come with me to more festive places reserved for guests of your stature."

Archibald followed him. Da'Żern remained near; Ribée and Grág made up the rear. Soldiers with spears sleek and long guarded entranceways, their armor burnished bronze, and their capes like the surf. Their eyes were hidden behind visors, their mouths clamped in silent obedience.

"As esteemed guests, you have a selection of bedchambers to best suit your needs. My stewards are at your beck, but I'll not feel slighted if you wish to use your own."

"How generous of you. 'Twill be mine own soldiers and servants I use. I trust they'll arrive from their climb soon?"

"Very soon, I assure you. I wished to meet you privily, and certainly so after the word we'd received from Spęèl."

"Spęèl." Archibald darkened. "What did they write?"

"'Tis of great import. They say you killed their chieftain and several of his servants. Is this so?"

"It is."

93

"Why would a king kill his own underling?"

"Is *that* what concerns you?" asked Archibald.

"You've asked for our naval forces. Should we give them to you after such blatant treachery?"

"You're misinformed, Emperor Bosker. 'Twas *they* first betrayed *me*."

"*They?* But the letter—"

"—is part of their plot against me. Emperor Bosker, 'tis Kendalan custom to feast when visiting. Both parties must present food or drink. They prepared a feast, and I offered tiger bone wine. We ate and drank together, sealing the peace between us."

The false emperor furrowed his brow. "Then why this letter?"

"*They* attempted to poison *me*. When those attempts failed, they sought to imprison me. Da'Żern is my trusted protector. He saw their deeds and defended me."

Da'Żern nodded. *Happily, without hesitation.*

Archibald continued. "After that, they tried to murder me outright. We made our escape. Our ship is larger, faster, and my crew is better armed besides. They could not fight us—but they knew *you* could."

"So, we would turn you away, kill you for fear of betrayal, or hold you for them?"

"Precisely, my friend!"

The false emperor was unmoved. "And how do we know you speak true? 'Tis your word against the Spęèlosi's. They call you a raving, murderous madman. What is *their* motive?"

"What is mine? I am of sound mind. I raved not. I raised no sword to them, and I spilled no Spęèlo blood. Their motive is clear. They seek independence and were willing to rebel. Instead of treating peacefully, they decided to attempt my life."

"And this behavior was hitherto unknown? They made no such pleas beforehand?"

"I assure you, they did not."

"Will you war with them?"

"Would you rather I did nothing? Mayhap I should allow them to continue their own rebellion across the seas that they might make more attempts on my life? If they came to me in peace, I would have heard them, perhaps allowed them their independence. That they have asked not with tongue but an assassin's dagger, it would not be meet to allow them to continue living."

Bosker the False fell silent until he finally said, "Yes, we sovereigns must keep up appearances. If rebellions are not quickly quelled, we face problems bigger. Your decision was a wise one. I do hope you reach your goals safely."

*And yet you offer none of your own men. It matters not. Tourm is what I've come for, and Tourm is of the greatest import.* "Speaking of lingering, it appears we've again taken your corridor for our field room. Please, to your solar, your throne room, aught."

"Yes." Bosker smiled, laughed. "You are correct. We've many matters to discuss. But before all that, I wish you'd come with me to the great hall. My cooks have prepared a wondrous meal."

Archibald frowned. "Very well, although I would like to com-mence—"

"And we shall, on the morrow. No doubt you're tired from the long journey here. I know there are some Stonehill dishes you'd like to try, and I am fascinated by this tiger bone wine."

Dourly, Archibald withdrew a wineskin from his robe. "I always carry some on my person. I warn you, though: 'tis a bitter, sour thing."

"Well enough, bitter though it may be, it is still a delicacy of your land. And I do not want to insult the custom of sharing drink. Please, come this way."

The glances the false emperor cast were mistrusting but it mattered little. Archibald had arrived safely at Stonehill. His grandfather had returned once more. Soon Tourm would be his.

# 6: The Impossible War

Archibald paced his room. He walked three steps—never more and never less—turned and began again. He was growing impatient, weary. He needed surcease from his own mind, and there was naught within the bedchamber but the increasing worry of being alone.

He tried to remind himself he wasn't alone, that da'Żern, al'Foyl, and Commons waited right outside the door. But the door was in the way. How should he know what the opposite side hid?

Could it be they were dead?

Or worse, that they had abandoned him?

Archibald cursed every moment one of his servants hesitated to do something. Hesitation meant weakness, betrayal.

Still pacing, he looked to the ceiling. Sheets of fine, translucent silk the color of seafoam hung from the stalactites and drew over his bed like a spider's web.

*The ceiling is too high. How is a man supposed to feel safe when the ceilings are so tall? They rise high enough to suffocate me!*

*That is what it is,* Archibald thought. *A trap, a means of suffocation.*

There was no one he trusted outside those doors. Bosker probably had his soldiers killed, his ship sunk. No doubt that a cruel false emperor would keep Archibald locked within this room without food or drink. He would perish, alone. He stopped mid-step, if only for a moment.

*When* was *the last time I received a meal?*

Was he hungry or full? When did he last eat? When did he last sleep? How long has it been since he last saw the sun?

*Years ago*, a voice decided.

Another said: *Decades.*

Everything was dead—past dead—dust.

The war was long over. Tourm had won, invaded Kendala, claiming it because he had been gone for so long.

But what did that make him? Was that all he was? Gone?

Had that false emperor killed him? Was this cavernous bed-chamber part of the Under Realms? Or perhaps it was only a vestibule, a place he was meant to wait in whilst the overgods decided his judgment?

*Do my ancestors argue with whatever overgods would hear? Do they plead for my freedom?*

And then another thought crossed his mind.

*What if I am not dead?*

What if, at that last meal—whenever it truly was—he poisoned me with something known only to the Stonehill poisoners? That poison would keep him alive, forever, as the world passed without him.

Was that the false emperor's ploy, to keep Archibald as a pet? A trophy? Something to watch, to gawk at, to show off to whatever courtesans might come calling?

*Get a look at the false king of Kendala*, Bosker would tell the drooling, stupid masses. *Come see the man who thought he could claim the great nation of Tourm! Come see the man who thought the* greater *nation of Stonehill would help him!*

The thought impressed a deep frown on his face. His eyes slowly crept along the stone chamber he resided in.

A knock at the wooden door made him stop, turn.

*How can this be? I am alone.*

"Come," he demanded.

The door opened and in stepped da'Żern, al'Foyl, and Commons.

Their silken capes, like green and blue ghosts, trailed da'Żern and al'Foyl, respectively.

All three of them bowed. Archibald felt relieved. However, it was a sensation most fleeting. Behind the three came seven knights belonging to Bosker.

Archibald choked. "What is the meaning of this?"

"Forgive our lateness, Eminence," said the Forest Dancer. "The Emperor has sent these men as escorts—"

"Escorts?" Archibald's vision yellowed with venom. "To *where*, da'Żern?"

"The field room." If da'Żern heard the animosity, he made no notice of it. "Emperor Bosker wishes to discuss the invasion with you. After last night's meal, you made your case plain."

"Last night?"

A shadow of concern flickered over Da'Żern's face. He stepped closer to Archibald, brought his voice low. "Do you not remember any of it?"

"No."

Da'Żern looked confused. "We feasted in your honor."

Archibald raised his fingers, and his faithful soldier quieted. He looked to the seven Stonehill soldiers. "Gentlemen, of course!"

he said loudly, a wide grin on his face. "Lead the way, please! I trust not only the Emperor, but his finest commanders will be there as well!"

Then he turned to da'Żern and whispered, "Walk with me that you may tell me all I said last night." Even saying it felt like ashes in his mouth.

"I will, Eminence, but first you may wish to change out of your clothes."

Archibald darkened. "I'll *not* meet the Emperor nude, you—"

"No, Eminence, I meant—" da'Żern stepped closer and whispered, "These are your clothes from yesterday, the ones you wore to supper. You may wish to change them, perhaps refresh yourself in your basin?"

Archibald frowned, but his anger receded. "I shall."

"Did you even sleep last night, Your Eminence?"

"I did, but perhaps I am more tired than I realized. I hadn't even prepared for bed. Give me peace and summon my steward."

As the knights waited outside, the steward entered. He was washed and had his hair combed back by the boy. He put on a nice robe of green, with a belt and slippers of gold-cloth. He examined himself in a mirror, pleased but for bags under his eyes. He reassumed his vapid expression and went into the hall to join the others.

The seven knights, dressed in shining bronze armor and capes as fluid as the sea, led the four Kendalans down the cavernous corridor of carved rock. Archibald remained in the back, with da'Żern.

"Speak not false and relate mine actions."

"Do you truly not remember?"

"Does it matter if I remember or not?" he hissed. "I gave you an order. I'll hear only the retelling—naught else."

"Yes, Your Eminence. The meal was a wonderful one, a good bounty from the sea. Shellfish, mostly: Giant frost crabs, spider shrimp poached in butter, fried pipefish with-"

"I asked not what we *had*," Archibald snapped. "I asked what we *discussed*."

"I thought you'd like to know in case Emperor Bosker questions you about it."

Archibald puckered his lips, thinking about Da'Żern's words. "Very well, but tarry not with it. Was it all delicious?"

"Yes, it was."

"And what did Bosker think of the tiger bone wine?"

"He called it an acquired taste, stating they had no flavors to compare it with. He did finish one goblet, though refused a second. I don't believe he approved."

Archibald nodded. Kendala used brine and vinegar in their food. A summertime favorite is the sour plum. Archibald was not surprised to know that Stonehill did not eat many sour things, but he was happy that Bosker had been good enough to finish his wine. "Good. Now, what did we discuss?"

"Emperor Bosker asked about Tourm, about Kendala's history with war. You spoke of how our nation thrived from a simple country whose surroundings were forests, rice paddies, and marshlands, and how we grew into the mighty nation. Mostly you spoke of Kendala's skirmishes with Tourm, past, and present."

"That must have taken hours."

"It did, in fact," said da'Żern. He could not hide his worried look. "But the Emperor seemed otherwise at ease, and there were enough courses for the telling."

Archibald raised his eyebrows. "At ease?"

"He was happy receiving an account of Kendala's history from its king. 'Who else would know better?' he asked."

"I see. What else was mentioned?"

Da'Żern knew what Archibald asked. He cleared his throat and shifted his gaze. "The, ah, incident at the archipelago."

"Yes?"

"I think you handled it well."

*Again, he hesitates. Because he lies.* "How?"

"First, you mentioned the belief that Kendalans came from the archipelago after the Sundering of the Stones. Seeing the kingdoms upon that land in ruins, we took it and claimed it for ourselves. Our kingdom was small, of course, but we thrived due to the—"

"Yes, da'Żern, I know the tale. I've enough Kendalan pride to fill this entire palace. What I know *not* is what was said regarding the archipelago."

"Yes, well, he brought up the incident. It was not a happy retelling. You again accused them of rebelling, of seeking to do what our ancestors had done—reclaim the mainland for themselves. You said they are attempting to slander your name, to do whatever they could to disrupt the meeting with Stonehill. You even went so far as to say that when Kendala is conquered, the Falawyspi will attack Stonehill—"

"And they *will*, da'Żern." Archibald looked ahead. Al'Foyl and Commons walked in front, following the seven soldiers. It did not appear as though they watched them, so he whispered again. "Did Bosker say aught against me?"

"Nothing more than what was discussed before supper. He listened intensely, wished to know more about their culture and Kendala's past with them. I believe you answered all quite tactfully."

"No doubt I did. Tell me: What was discussed for the invasion?"

"Of Tourm?"

"No, fool, of Falawyspa."

"Why would we invade them? They're—"

"Have you not been listening? They attempted to assassinate me!"

"Yes, I remember. But why would Stonehill aid the invasion against the archipelago? 'Tis Tourm you seek. Once you've their forces, they'll be no need of Stonehill's fleet."

Archibald darkened, but relented. "You've a fair point. One final question before we arrive: Did I convince them to lend me their fleets?"

"We travel to their field room now."

"In his letter to me, Bosker stated that he wished to hear of the struggles we faced. But there is more to it than that. We must make them aware of the benefits allying with us presents. Did I do that?"

"I—" But he silenced himself when the soldiers turned.

"We're arrived at the field room," said al'Foyl.

Archibald frowned. He had not heard the entire truth from da'Żern, and yet he knew he could not keep the false emperor waiting by requesting to remain outside as he spoke with da'Żern. *He already distrusts me for those damned islanders.* So, he waved his arm and said, "Allow us in."

The room was as large as Archibald's bedchambers, perhaps larger. In the center was a large table of stone, cut into a perfect circle. Upon it was a map, a large cross shape laden with mountains, hills, forests, lakes, rivers and streams, and cities and towns. The northeast appendage, however, was bare and barren, flat gray stone when all the others had been painted. In the center of the cross-shaped continent was a large and craggy mountain, rising to a point like a single earthen fang. Overseer Mountain, Bosker had called it.

Stonecephar's field room only contained a map of the Holy Lands.

"Welcome, King Archibald!" Bosker entered the room with Ribée, sharp-nosed and watery-eyed, and the strong, stoic, silent Grág.

With them came two figures Archibald did not know. One of them was tall and wiry, with a full head of hair, the makings of a fine beard, and robes of royal purple silk. The man next to him was taller, with a squat nose, small eyes, and deep-set frown one might make if they stepped into a room of ordure.

"Good morn, Your Imperial Majesty."

Bosker grinned wide. His teeth looked like stark white pebbles upon a sandy beach. "You remember Ribée and Grág, do you not?"

"I do," said Archibald. "It has been but a few hours."

"Ah, of course. Well, here we've my younger brother, Argoff. He is the Archduke of Stonecephar and my closest confidant. Next to him is Grág's younger brother, Drág Enoź, castellan of Stonecephar Palace."

"A pleasure, Argoff, and Drág. Forgive my nescience, but why are the archduke and the castellan present? They seem ill-suited to discuss maritime strategies. An admiral would be a better substitute."

"Have you no trusted advisors?" Bosker asked pleasantly. Torchlight shined from the sconces in the cavern walls. He appeared golden in their light. "You travel yet with da'Żern, al'Foyl, and Commons. Certainly, there are more you've had to leave behind. Well—" his voice sharpened "—these are *mine* and all of them are *here*. Worry not, though: the admiral comes. She merely ran late this morn."

"Very well; and where shall I and my men stand?"

"There, if you please."

Archibald, da'Żern, al'Foyl, and Commons moved to where the

false emperor gestured. He looked down upon the northwest corner, gray and empty. There were no forests, no mountains, and no bodies of water.

"Unfinished, I see," al'Foyl commented.

Archibald could have slapped him for his impertinence. Or at least, da'Żern could do it. *Best never to muddy your own hands.*

Bosker seemed not to mind: his voice was calm. "That is Argineld, where none have ever been."

"I recall," said Archibald, still looking at the gray slab. "The pages of your history say naught regarding the battle that ensued, same as the pages of your tomes."

"One thing remains certain," said Bosker, still smiling. "We lost."

"Piteous, that. But surely you must have tried other methods of breaching the land. By sea, for instance."

"We have, but for naught. Tales mention ships left but never returned. It might be sheer cliffs surround the area, or it could be the same galawhale that guards Deluga."

"What *is* the galawhale?"

"A man-eating leviathan covered in armorlike plates. It destroys vessels—cogs, galleys, and aught in between. It but dwells in the northwest, Deluga's Crystal Reef. Never has it interfered with the fishermen or navy of Stonehill." Bosker looked at Deluga, its mountain ranges covered with white. Snowfields interspersed with green forests, and the very tip was steely gray and flat, like ice. He smiled again. "Now *that*, Archibald, is in the tomes."

Archibald winced. He hated hearing his name without a title before it. He recovered and asked, "Are they?"

Bosker nodded, smiling. "During the campaign centuries ago, we sent our men through the mountains. We tried to send our navy as well. Ten galleys left that morn, and none returned."

"How do you know what it was?" asked al'Foyl.

"There were witnesses," said a new voice. "And we learned of the galawhale from the locals too late."

A new woman stood in front. She wore no armor, but a doublet of shimmering cerulean. Her blond hair was tightly braided. Behind her were other men, some younger, stouter, all looking crusty and calloused from the sea.

"Ah!" exclaimed the Emperor, clapping his hands together. "Admiral Corinna Bellamy, how good of you to come!"

"Late though you are," sniffed Archibald.

"'Late though I'—" The Admiral turned to Bosker. "Who the scump does he think he is?"

"Be at peace," said Bosker. "This is King Archibald, the man I mentioned who is in grievous need of our—*your*—navy."

Admiral Bellamy wrinkled her nose and stood next to her emperor. The gaggle of grim captains followed. Archibald's eyes did not leave the admiral's, yet he could feel how alone he was compared to the Stonehillers. The emperor, false though he was, surrounded himself with strong leaders, and looked formidable himself.

Archibald, on the other hand, only had three soldiers with him, and one of them a boy still in training. He did not know if his other soldiers alighted in the palace or the town below, but he wished they were with him.

"So," grunted Bellamy, "where's the map, Kendalan King?"

"The map?"

She sighed. "Of Fangaard? Or Tourm? We know not the route, nor the lay of the land, nor the areas which we may attack. You need a map."

"No doubt we've something of the sort," Archibald said. He turned to Da'Żern. "Where are our maps?"

Da'Żern hesitated, eyes darting about. "Unless one of the other soldiers thought wisely, they remain within the *King's Glory*."

Archibald closed his eyes tightly and exhaled. Raising his voice would get him nowhere. Neither would it do to kill da'Żern. He looked at that insolent admiral, and said, "Can we, for the time being, negate the maps from our plot?"

"Planning strategies is difficult without them," said Bellamy. "And difficult, too, would it make returning to your realm."

"They are not presently with us. If truly we are bereft, your ships can follow mine." Archibald sneered. "All you must do is tell your men I hold sway over them until the war is won. You needn't come back with me, Admiral."

"But I insist," said Bellamy. Her face was blank, her mouth a hard line neither smiling nor frowning. Archibald could see her eyes dancing with malicious fire. "I would not leave my men to one so inexperienced."

Archibald snarled. "You *dare* deny me?"

"Stay yourself, Archibald," growled Bosker, one hand aloft. "Bellamy speaks true. Your methods may have kept you alive, if naught else. But they shan't win you this war."

"What mean you?"

"Is that not why you're come? To win the impossible war you've made for yourself?"

Bosker stepped around the table, toward Archibald. The seven soldiers followed, which made him nervous. Behind him, Da'Żern and al'Foyl readied their weapons. He was glad they were there, and gladder still they had armed themselves not just with their weapons, but with their spear-mail as well.

111

"I recall your message's words," said Bosker. "You sounded utterly desperate. Your ramblings last night confirmed for me one thing: the gain you seek is wholly for yourself, no matter the lies you tell me or your own men."

"What do you imply?"

"That you're ill-suited to win this war," said Bellamy. "You're brash, dependent on your soldiers, and a terrible strategist besides."

Bosker smiled. "If you wish to win and claim Tourm as your own, you'd be wise to give *your* men to *my* commanders. Worry not; we shall win this war for you."

"What slight is this?"

"No slight, Archibald." Bosker's cold familiarity wounded him. "Your men are brave, strong, and capable. But lack they proper discipline. And proper discipline is brought by a proper leader. Fear not, for at the backs of your men shall be the strategists of Stonehill. Victory is promised, secured!"

"For whom?"

"Stop this, Archibald," Bosker said firmly. "You act the child. Save yourself the embarrassment."

That dangerous flash reentered his eyes, but Archibald did not care. "I am *not* acting the child! Give my soldiers to you, and you would turn around and see Kendala added to your false empire!"

That took him back. "False?" He shook his head. "I know not what you mean."

"You claim to be Emperor of the Holy Lands, but you can longer bring your men into Deluga or Flamburg! And you've never stepped foot in Argineld. You rule only Stonehill! Your empire *is* false but shall no longer be once you've killed me and claimed Tourm and Kendala both!"

"Your words cut deep," said Bosker, eyes smoldering. His voice was dark and deep, but calm. "Leave now. You'll have no further aid from Stonehill."

"No."

Bosker raised his eyebrows. "*No?* You, worthless fool of a king, have upset your host!" He crossed the room in quick strides, coming nose to nose with Archibald. "You have spat upon mine offer and hospitality. Leave *now* or ne'er return to your kingdom—which sounds copious enough without *claiming* another, for there's naught to reclaim. That war was hundreds of years ago. Your ancestors' claims perished at their deaths. Count your losses and pull your men from Tourm—"

Archibald's fist slammed against Bosker's chin, knocking him aside.

Da'Żern and al'Foyl rushed forward, shoving their King behind them. Al'Foyl called to Commons, "Get to the ship!"

The seven Stonehill soldiers ran forth, drawing their swords.

Da'Żern and al'Foyl were too fast for them. Da'Żern slashed through their flesh, cut their faces and necks with his duel-bladed polearm.

"There's no time to watch!" Commons shouted over the din. "We must away!"

"But my navy!" Archibald cried, just as al'Foyl dispatched a captain.

"I'd say that ship has sailed," said Commons. "*C'mon!*"

Archibald relented, following the lad down the stonewalled corridors. There were places on the floor that opened to become shallow pools. Stalactites dripped water down upon them, wetting the reflective tiles. How Archibald could have thought something so natural was beautiful was beyond him.

*Bosker was indeed a false emperor*, he thought. *No one of prideful birth would confine himself to a cave.*

Commons stopped and looked about. The path branched off into several tunnels. "Where now?"

"You know not the way?" asked Archibald.

"Er—*left!*"

They ran down the leftmost path, the horrors of the field room becoming more distant. Da'Żern, sometimes hesitant and other times foolish, was a good soldier, nonetheless. Yet again, he and al'Foyl fought to protect him. They would die for him but from afar. The only protection Archibald had now was the urchin, Commons.

"Right," said Commons, and he followed.

But they found soldiers, armed with tridents and short swords, armored in bronze with sweeping capes the color of the sea. Commons gasped and shrunk away, but it did no good. Perhaps they heard his gasp, or perhaps saw his shadow. The bronze-armored soldiers found them.

"King Archibald!" one of them gasped. "Shouldn't you be in the field room with Emperor Bosker?"

"The meeting has sojourned," Archibald lied. "I go to my ship to prepare for departure. The navy follows soon thereafter."

From behind the bronze helm, Archibald saw his eyes blinking, his brain working. At last, the stupid knight said, "Wouldn't it be easier to follow you from the port?"

"I have provided a map. 'Twill be of no consequence to follow me."

"Oh," said the guardsmen. He turned to his brigade when another stepped forward.

"Did you not travel with *three* bodyguards instead of one?"

That paused him. He was trying to return to his ship without *any* of his soldiers or stewards.

But a third lie came to him. "They prepare with Admiral Bellamy. They're to be escorted down later, I'm certain."

"Your Eminence!" rang a voice from behind.

Archibald turned, surprised to see da'Żern and al'Foyl running toward them. His eyes widened. They were covered in leaking cuts; their weapons dripped crimson. Nicks marked their armor, and their silken capes were tattered.

Archibald tried to think up another lie, something to explain their disheveled states before the guards could see them and raise more questions. Alas, the only thing Archibald could think was curses. *Would that they had died*!

Da'Żern and al'Foyl finally met them, out of breath. The brigade captain stepped forward, eyes wide behind his visor's slits. "What's happened?" His hand gripped the sword at his side, but he did not draw.

Da'Żern saw the soldier's hand and lunged. The captain pulled the sword free, but Da'Żern's bloody blades slashed the man down. The others came with their tridents, and al'Foyl rushed in. The Kendalan armor had been designed for such weapons. The tips bounced away from their armor and let the two get closer for the kill. Even Commons joined in, using his battle fork with less skill perhaps, but enough fervidity to match the others.

Soon the brigade was dead. They came away wounded further, but nothing so much that their lives felt threatened.

Now in the lead, they all followed da'Żern. "We could never scale the mountain," he said. "We must trick the skałagad keeper to let us down. More soldiers follow. We must hurry."

"A task difficult should our wounds and tattered clothes come into question," said al'Foyl.

"Belike, they will," huffed da'Żern.

"If only all of Stonehill was not so suspicious," Archibald said. "I nearly had that brigade fooled! They would've escorted Commons and I to the skałagady keeper themselves had you not arrived so bloody."

"Keep low your voice," said al'Foyl. "We all wish to escape with our lives!"

"Yes," said Commons, "but what about—?"

"He means to leave them," da'Żern answered.

Commons gasped, but al'Foyl explained. "It is the right thing. We risk torture, perhaps death ourselves if we go back for the servants and stewards."

"That isn't right."

"We are warriors, Markí, sworn to protect King Archibald no

117

matter the price, even if it comes at our own lives."

"Ours is not to reason," muttered da'Żern. "Ours is to act."

"At least if we survive, we can make certain their family shrines receive blessed figurines," said Archibald. "Besides, the carriages only hold four people, which is us."

They wandered through the cavernous halls for some time, but Archibald insisted they stop at a nearby pool to wash the blood from their skin and strip their tattered capes for makeshift bandages. Al'Foyl shared the remnants of his with Commons. They discarded the remains.

Paces quickened, they moved about the halls. Brigades marching through stopped for some words, but never long enough to question the King and his soldiers. Archibald did not doubt the Stonehillers pursued them, but it was apparently not yet known throughout Stonecephar Palace.

Finally—happily—they found the old, gnarled man that tended the skałagady, right at the wide vestibule that opened into blue oblivion. Archibald came to him, tried his damnedest not to grasp him. "My bodyguards and I wish to go down *now*."

"Down?" the old man asked, slowly. "To where?"

"To *King's Glory*—my ship."

The old man peered at all four of them. "Are the meetings over? You've reached an agreement?"

"We have, we have!" said Archibald, rolling his hand around. "All is well, we are not leaving. I only wish to inform my captain and crew. Of course, my bodyguards accompany me, but my stewards remain behind."

"Couldn't you send a bird—?"

"This I would quite rather do myself," Archibald hissed. "Now let us down, lest Emperor Bosker hears how I was accosted!"

The keeper hurried into a small chamber in the right wall and came out with a coachman dressed in royal blue, filigreed with yellow piping. The four Kendalans climbed into the coach pulled by two skałagadi. Though nowhere near as ornate as the one they had used to climb up the mountain, the King supposed comfort mattered little when lives were on the line.

The coachman slipped into the driver's station and took up the reins. Soon, the dragons were on their way down the mountainside. They had managed to escape from the hostile Stonehillers. They now made their way homeward. All that was left to do was give the command to hoist anchor. *King's Glory* would be seaborne.

*Let us be gone from Stonehill once and for all.*

*Or would you be?*

Eyes wide, Archibald lurched forward. Da'Żern was in front of him, his mouth moving uselessly. "Grandfather?"

*'Twas their navy you sought, and their navy you shall receive, but not the same that you wished of it.*

"What mean you, Grandfather?"

*Ask it not of me. Know you already the answer.*

His grandfather's hoary face would not appear. All he could see was da'Żern's flapping tongue, mouth opening, and closing, eyes wide with fright. He reached out and touched it. "Stop, you look a landed fished."

Suddenly, a new voice entered his mind, young and haughty—a sneering voice he feared and knew all too well.

*You will lead them to their dooms!*

"*Your Eminence!*"

Archibald shook his head, dazed. "Al'Foyl—?"

"You look unwell," said the Water Dancer. "You were no longer with us."

"What nonsense, al'Foyl. I am *always* with you—just as my grandfather is ever with me."

The skałagady pulled to a halt. The smell of sea air pervaded their nostrils. Buildings of sandstone dotted the view—houses and huts and places of business, all by the sea. The coachman opened the door, and the four soldiers scrambled out before their king. Their eyes darted every-which-way, and so did Archibald's. There seemed to be no sign of the Stonehillers, and *King's Glory* was right ahead of them, gangplank lowered.

Archibald licked his lips when he saw it but did not stare too long. He put a gold coin into the coachman's hand and said, "Wait here, we'll be only but a moment."

Of course, he would never return.

Surrounded by his guard, Archibald walked to the gangplank as quickly as he could. He was perhaps halfway up the shaking board when someone called from behind: "*Stop them!*"

Archibald looked behind him. Bronze-plated men charged with spears, swords, and bows and arrows. No doubt word had reached the Stoneport city watch. It mattered not, for they were free. Archibald joined the rest on deck. As da'Żern and al'Foyl raised the gangplank, Captain Welmá met them.

"Your Eminence—a nice surprise but a surprise nonetheless!" He eyed the two soldiers hoisting the gangplank, heard the cries coming from the approaching foemen. "What—?"

"No time for questions. Hoist anchor. We sail *now!*"

Welmá commanded the deckhands to do so.

Arrows sailed above their heads. Hooked ladders bounced onto the gunwale. "The Stonehillers are trying to board!" Soldiers went to them.

The sun dampened as the sails unfurled. Little *plunks*, splashes of water, filled his ears. *Good*, thought the King, *the oars are dropped.*

With the last slash of rope, *King's Glory* was free. With sails unfurled and oars in the water, they pulled out of port. Those hooked siege ladders were useless, but the arrows continued to fly. Several smacked into the deck, others soared harmlessly overhead.

Commons, al'Foyl, and da'Żern waited near the captain's cabin. Da'Żern moved closer to him, sweating. The silken strips of green dripped red from the blood underneath. "Come, Eminence, you must—"

His eyes widened as he pushed Archibald down.

A choke and a spray of blood. An arrow shot through da'Żern's throat, emerging from the other side with an explosion of meat. His eyes widened, but he fell to the ground. His tongue lolled uselessly in his mouth as he struggled to breathe, but he found no quarter with the Goddess of Air.

Al'Foyl was there, suddenly, bending over him, leading him indoors. Besides the scratches and scars, his armor also carried three arrows. "Inside!" he shouted, as another arrow thudded into his spear-mail.

Al'Foyl closed the door behind them, signing deeply. "A pity for da'Żern."

"Da'Żern. Yes, a pity. He was a good soldier. He gave his life for his king." He smiled. *And happily, he did not hesitate to do so.*

He looked through the small window. The Stonehillers launched fire arrows. Flames snapped at the wood. They would need to be extinguished, but perhaps when the foemen could no longer reach them.

"Eminence?"

Archibald faced the Water Dancer. "Bosker—that false emperor—must have given word that we meant to escape. 'Twas the city watch that attacked us, not the emperor's own men. The admiral and all the captains could not pursue. They remained in Stonecephar."

"You needn't have called him false," said Commons.

Archibald noticed the boy had tears in his eyes. He frowned at them, took the boy by the chin, forcing his eyes to his own.

"Now you know the price a dancer must pay. Da'Żern gave his life for his king. He did as he learned. Those left behind shall be questioned, tortured. We must send two letters with our swiftest wings."

"What?" Al'Foyl looked surprised. "What would they say?"

"Tourm is not our enemy, as we have been led to believe. I now see my mistake, al'Foyl."

"Their slights against Kendala—"

"We'll have our land returned to us, mark my words. But we've spilled Stonehiller blood. We've insulted their sovereign. Once they've the information from those left behind, they shall pursue. Are you ready for the message?"

Al'Foyl nodded.

The next part pained him to say. "Send the first letter to Kóń ka'Glęz. He is to relinquish Tourm's Gate and pull all men back to Zachwalaç."

"And the second, Eminence?"

Archibald's jaw tightened, but there was little he could do for it. "The second goes to King Biel. Tell him I wish to sue for peace. We now war against Stonehill."

# About the Author

Adam has loved fantasy since he was a kid, and medieval Eastern Europe enthralls him. He lives in Chicago where he sings in a band called "Sacred Monster" and practices Japanese swordsmanship. He enjoys playing guitar and is a devout follower of rock and metal music. He hopes to add his own twists to the world of fantasy with his first novel, turned series, "Wolves of War."

**You can connect with me on:**

https://privatedragon.com

# Also by Adam TS Conlon

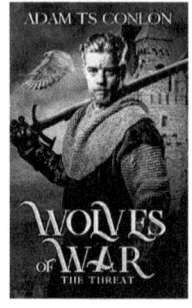

**Wolves of War: The Threat**
**The collapse of peace is inevitable.**

The kingdom of Tourm has enjoyed peace for fifty years, but the head that wears the crown grows feeble. Unrest rules inside the kingdom and border skirmishes have become common. The nation of Kendala to the south marches on Tourm. The frantic masses whisper... war.

Read an authentic tale of Orrick pan Pallaton by Adam TS Conlon.

This is a brutal story of duty and triumph in a fantastic adventure. Orrick is a new knight and untested; he must find grit to face deadly challenges on and off the battlefield. Political schemes and dangers in the dark threaten him, while others would like him dead.

**The kingdom of Tourm is in turmoil, and Orrick must discover the meaning of valor to survive.**

### Wolves of War: Storm and Siege

Attacked and outnumbered upon arriving in Kendala, Tourm's small, peaceful envoy is forced to flee through the expansive Sea of Trees. Ambushed and afraid, they are unable to send word to the Crown regarding Kendala's betrayal. While they are hounded by monsters and highwaymen, the Kendalan army—led by their new power-mad monarch—strikes the seaside duchy of Nin. With their land conquered, the royal family struggles to maintain control. The King is unsure. The Crown Prince worries. Citizens panic. Warrior guilds, thirsty for blood and hungry for gold, squabble for a chance at the frontlines. Amidst total war, Orrick looks to his senior officers for guidance. But not all enemies fight under foreign banners, and blood washes away naught but disgrace. Relishing in violence, killing to reclaim Nin, can Orrick balance valor and bloodlust, or will madness and betrayal tear him apart?